TRAPPED IN
HALF
POSITION

TRAPPED IN HALF POSITION

BY DIXIE HUTHMAKER

Avenine Press

Aventine Press
1023 4th Avenue, Suite 204
San Diego, CA 92101
ISBN: 1-59330-317-3

Printed in the United States of America

To Buddy, Anna and Charlie,
my greatest treasures.
You are simply the best.

&

To Colleen Moore DiGuilian,
who asked me the magic question:
"Who wants to play the violin?"

Acknowledgements

If you want to write, you must have a dream and a support team.

All my love and thanks go to my family: Buddy, Anna and Charles, who always dreamed with me, read, edited and, most of all, called me a writer.

Every writer needs a special writing friend. My friend is Mary Kay Remich who has shared the journey with me for twenty-plus years.

My gratitude to Dana Lowe, orchestra director extraordinaire, and Mike Nichols, gifted violist and teacher, who read, proofed and gave me words of encouragement.

And to all my students who gave me years of inspiration, amazement and music making, I thank you.

CHAPTER ONE ||

Anna slid lower in her chair, staring at the page of music and hoping that the music stand protected her from the teacher's attention. Around her, the Lincoln Junior High Orchestra rehearsed the *Brandenburg Concerto No.3* by Bach, unaware that Anna was lost.

"Anna, catch up," the orchestra director, Mrs. Sanders, called out over the music.

By the time Anna found the right spot in the music, the orchestra thundered past and she was lost, again. The group of young musicians was polishing the piece for their annual Thanksgiving assembly program. Anna pretended to play, trying to follow the two violists in front of her but their bows moved too quickly.

The director stopped conducting and the orchestra stopped—except for Mark Pointer, who kept playing, as usual.

"Mark? How many times do I have to tell you? Stop playing when I stop conducting," Mrs. Sanders said, glaring at the string bass player. The tone of the teacher's voice warned that Mark had played past the cut-off sign too many times during the morning's rehearsal.

"Anna," Mrs. Sanders said, turning her attention back to the viola section. "Tell me where you're having trouble so I can help you."

Squirming in her seat, Anna felt the stares of the older students. Of the forty-two students in the class, Anna was the youngest. She loved being in the orchestra but she didn't need all this extra attention.

"It's the half position," she answered. From measure forty-nine to measure fifty-two, she had to play in that weird position viola players used for passages with extra sharps. She had to shift her hand backwards about half an inch, play six notes, and then shift back. It sounded easy—and it was for everyone but Anna.

"Do you have the fingerings marked?" Mrs. Sanders asked.

"It's not the fingerings. I get in half position and I play the notes—but I can't get out of half position."

Cristin Lang, the violist who sat in front of Anna, turned around and grinned, her brown eyes magnified behind owl-eyed glasses. "Trapped in half position. What a way to go."

"At least we won't have to look at her ugly face any more," Mark Pointer said. The rest of the class laughed at his remark.

"Drop dead, pea-brain," Cristin said, coming to her friend's rescue.

Anna's toes curled up inside her shoes as she fought against the telltale burning sensation that spread over her face. It never failed. Mark always found a way to make her the laughing stock of the class—like last week when he put the two-sided tape in the bottom of her chair. And when he picked on her, she always cowered in her seat, her face turning beet-red as she died inwardly.

Now she clinched her teeth together, wishing she had the courage to tell Mark to go look in the mirror if he wanted to see the ugliest face in the universe.

"Mark," the teacher said. "Apologize to Anna right now."

"What for?"

"Now." Mrs. Sanders had tons of patience with the young musicians. However, Mark required more than his share. Mrs.

Sanders once said that all of her gray hairs, which were not that noticeable, had Mark's name on them.

The gangly seventh grader sneered at Anna. "Sorry."

But she knew he wasn't. Not really. His favorite hobby was tormenting Anna. And, as the teacher turned her attention back to the orchestra class, he leaned over and whispered, "I'll get you after class, booby-trap."

Mrs. Sanders picked up her baton and tapped on the music stand for attention. "Start at measure sixty-four. And don't forget the crescendo."

The orchestra came to life again and Anna played, delighted to skip over the half position measures. As each section of the orchestra played Bach's version of musical "tag," Anna concentrated, listening to how her part blended with the rest of the group. *The Brandenburg* was a tough piece of music, Anna's favorite. Time flew by with the notes and after the group played through *Jazz Pizzicato*, the rehearsal ended.

"Don't forget All-City rehearsal tonight," Mrs. Sanders announced before the young musicians started putting their instruments away.

Anna loosened her bow and snapped it in the case. All-City Youth Orchestra. If only she were thirteen years old, she could audition for the group. A real symphony orchestra with strings, woodwind and brass instruments, All-City performed exciting music by Mozart, Bach, Beethoven and occasionally a fun piece from a Broadway musical. And every violist in the Lincoln Junior High Orchestra played in All-City—every violist but Anna.

"What music are you rehearsing tonight?" she asked Cristin.

"We got some neat new Christmas music. Wait until you hear it." Then Cristin's eyes widened. "Hey, why don't you come to rehearsal with me tonight?"

Anna carefully wiped the rosin from the strings of her viola. She wanted to go, but not to listen. She wanted to play. She wanted to be a member of the orchestra.

Cristin didn't wait for Anna's answer. "Did you hear the news? We're getting new uniforms for the trip. Dark blue long skirts and blazers."

Startled, Anna looked up at her best friend. Uniforms and a trip?

"Can you believe it? We're going to play at Disney World during Spring Break." Cristin's grin faded as she saw the look on Anna's face. "I wish you were going. We could be roommates."

But Anna wouldn't be thirteen until June. And All-City Orchestra was going to Disney World in April. Why did she have to wait until next year to audition? Being twelve was a major obstacle to the better things in life.

When the bell rang, Anna picked up her viola case and reached for her music folder. At that moment, Mark Pointer walked by, deliberately knocking her folder to the floor.

Music scattered everywhere. Her *Blue Grass Hoe-down* landed under Cristin's chair and *Silver Bells* floated all the way past the cello section. Then he stepped on her practice record sheet, leaving a dirty waffle print of his tennis shoe across the bottom of the page.

"You don't need to know anything about All-City," Mark said. "They don't let nerdy children like you in our orchestra."

Scrambling to pick up the music, Anna wished Mark Pointer could be shipped to the moon or to South America—with a one-way ticket. He tortured her every day, picking on her in front of the class until she felt like crawling under her chair from embarrassment. Collecting viola, music and books, she ran out the door to put the instrument in her locker.

Jinxed with a bottom locker, Anna squatted in the crowded hall, balancing books in her lap as she worked the combination lock. The Harry Potter poster taped on the inside of the locker door fell out. Anna grabbed at it before Harry was trampled by the student stampede moving down the hall.

The boy who opened the locker over hers waved at the air and muttered, "Phew" as he backed away. Her locker still reeked from the bottle of "Blue Gardenia" perfume that had spilled on her gym clothes last week. Stuffing her music folder beside the viola, she slammed the door and headed down the hall.

"Musk has to stay after school." Brent Norcross' singsong voice whined the chant over and over as the cello player caught up with her. In orchestra class, he sat on Anna's other side, trapping her between Mark and Brent. A monster sandwich with her as the filling.

Nicknamed the 'Pillsbury Dough Boy,' Brent looked the part with his dumpy jeans and T-shirts that never stayed tucked in. Brent copied whatever Mark Pointer said or did, which included making fun of Anna every chance he got. She tried to ignore the fat boy as she hurried to social studies class but he stuck to her like masking tape.

"Musk is trapped in half position," Brent said.

She hated to be called "Musk." It started in the sixth grade when Brent noticed that when Anna played, her hands sweated and left tiny puddles of water on the fingerboard of her viola.

"Gross," he had said.

Then, when Brent had to make a project for health class, he did a poster on keeping your hands clean and labeled the project, "MUSK: Mainly Un-Sanitary Kids." And he started calling Anna by the dreaded name.

She couldn't help it. She had sweaty hands. She tried blowing on them and wiping them on her jeans but nothing helped. Once she tried putting anti-perspirant on them. That didn't work either. Mrs. Sanders had told Anna that when she was a kid her hands had sweated too and that it went away as she got older. How old, Anna wondered? Thirteen? Fourteen? Twenty? Probably never.

"Did you leave a lake on your viola today?"

"Shut up, Brent." Looking straight ahead, Anna scooted into the social studies class as the tardy bell rang.

Two periods later, Anna was finishing a unit test in punctuation.

She stretched her legs and wished the lunch bell would ring so she could see Cristin again and hear more about All-City Orchestra.

Anna could imagine herself dressed in the long blue skirt and blazer, sitting on stage and playing Handel or Mozart. She didn't even care if she had to sit last chair in the viola section. She wanted to play.

Anna's stomach growled and gurgled, making the girl in the next desk snicker. Anna pushed at her stomach with her fist to make it stop but it growled again. In the quietness of language arts class, with everyone taking the test, it sounded like Leo the lion.

"P-s-s-s-t. Hey, you."

Anna looked up to find Elizabeth Jenkins hissing at her.

"Give this to Jenny," Elizabeth whispered, shoving a note at Anna.

Hey, you? Anna stared at the folded note in her hand. Two and a half months in the same class and Elizabeth still didn't know her name. But then why should she? Elizabeth and Jenny were the most popular girls in the seventh grade. They didn't know Anna existed—except to pass a note for them.

"Would you please give her the stupid note," Elizabeth whispered loudly. "Sometime this century?"

Anna checked to see if the teacher had heard. Miss Moore was writing the homework assignment on the board, her back turned to the class.

"My pleasure," Anna said to Elizabeth, knowing the moment the words escaped her mouth that she sounded dumb—definitely not cool like everything Elizabeth and Jenny said and did.

And everything they wore looked so terrific. They had had matching surfing T-shirts before anyone else had heard of the beach wear craze. And cool banana clips for their hair. If Elizabeth or Jenny got new mini-bags, soon the whole school would be at the mall buying mini-bags, same style, same color.

Their newest fad was colored tennis shoes. Jenny and Elizabeth met with all their friends after first period and traded shoes until everyone wore an unmatched pair. Today Jenny wore a pink shoe on her left foot and a blue one on her right. Elizabeth's were red and purple, and on Elizabeth's feet the strange color combination seemed to go together.

Under her desk, Anna wore a pair of ordinary, matching white tennis shoes.

Two rows over, Jenny watched Anna out of the corner of her eye, her hand extended beside the desk.

"Throw it," she whispered.

Without thinking, Anna tossed the note toward Jenny. The note took flight like a loony bird. It soared over Jenny's head and landed in the potted plant in the window. Anna stared at the note open-mouthed.

"Great shot, Musk," said Mark Pointer, who sat behind Jenny. "Two points." Then he laughed and the teacher turned around.

"Anna Browning?" Miss Moore stood in front of the class, her hands on her hips. "I'd like to talk to you."

Anna looked to Elizabeth but she pretended to be busy taking the test. No longer hungry, Anna felt queasy as she turned her paper face down and slid out of her desk. Heads popped up around the class to look at her as she made her way to the teacher's desk.

"Let's step out in the hall," the teacher said.

CHAPTER TWO ||

Anna's stomach turned somersaults. The teacher usually took students out of class to yell at them or to send them to the discipline office. Anna didn't even know where the discipline office was. What if they called her parents?

When the teacher closed the door, Anna started stammering. "I'm really sorry—I didn't mean—I mean I didn't think—"

"Anna, what are you talking about?" Miss Moore asked.

"The note," Anna said.

"What note? I wanted to talk to you about the spelling bee."

Anna exhaled slowly, the relief making her knees weak. Saved by the spelling bee.

Last week Anna had won the class spelling bee and was scheduled to be in the school contest on Friday. Orchestra won hands down as her favorite class but spelling ran a close second. After being district spelling champion for two years in elementary school, she planned that this year's match would make it three years in a row. She felt confident that she could beat the eighth and ninth graders easily. Then on to district competition.

"I'm afraid I've got some bad news," the teacher said. "The rules for junior high school state that all contestants must be thirteen years old by January 1."

Anna's mouth flew open as she guessed what was coming next.

"When the office checked your records, we were forced to disqualify you." The teacher shook her head slowly. "I'm sorry, Anna."

"But that's not fair," Anna said. "I won."

"I know and I'm very sorry."

"Can't they make an exception this time?" Anna pleaded. "I know all the vowel rules. I know when to ask for a definition. I've got experience."

The teacher patted her on the shoulder. "Anna, you're an excellent speller, the best I've had in years. If it's any consolation, you'll be able to compete next year."

Anna swallowed hard. Next year seemed light years away. What did the world have against twelve-year-olds? Surely, becoming a teen-ager would bring magical changes to her life—if she survived that long.

Head down, she returned to her desk. Elizabeth and Jenny didn't even look up when she sat down, and the note was no longer visible in the plant. Turning her test paper over, Anna tried to think about exclamation points, question marks and semi-colons instead of spelling bees. Who could concentrate when she had just been disqualified from one of the most important events in her life?

Life was not fair, Anna thought as she handed in her test.

As the class waited for the lunch bell to ring, Anna looked over at Jenny. Dressed in pink slacks and a matching sweater, Jenny read a paperback teen romance. Anna knew that Jenny and Elizabeth didn't care about playing in orchestras or winning spelling bees. Make-up, clothes and boys seemed to be all they talked about. The two girls rarely spoke to Anna, only when they had a question about math homework—or asked her to pass a note.

Anna felt positive that Elizabeth and Jenny had skipped over being twelve. And no one had ever dared to call them "Musk."

"It's called 'Cream of Yesterday'," Cristin explained to Brent, pointing to the gravy on his mashed potatoes. "The cafeteria workers take all the scrapings from yesterday's plates, put it all in a blender, add a little food coloring and—presto change-o—'Cream of Yesterday'."

Brent pushed his tray down the serving line, helping himself to an extra brownie. "I don't believe you for one minute. You're just making that up so I won't eat it."

Cristin shrugged and smiled. "It's your stomach."

Anna leaned over the counter to get a carton of milk, turning her face away from Brent before she started to giggle. Only Cristin could tell such a story with a straight face.

"Want your brownie?" Brent asked, poking his finger into the top of Cristin's dessert.

"Want to live past sundown?" Cristin said, her smile disappearing.

Brent held his lunch ticket out to the cashier. "I'm not sitting with you two. You'll find something else wrong with my lunch." He walked away from the serving line, his red T-shirt hanging out of the back of his jeans.

Anna and Cristin stood in the cafeteria, looking for a vacant table—far away from Brent. The noise level of the cafeteria sounded like a beehive as the maze of kids chattered and, unsuspecting, devoured 'Cream of Yesterday.'

As Elizabeth pushed past the two girls, Anna followed her to a table and started to pull out a chair.

"You can't sit here. These seats are saved," Elizabeth said.

A burning sensation spread over Anna's cheeks as she and Cristin slid their trays down to the next table.

"Miss Personality strikes again," Cristin said.

Four other girls plus Jenny quickly filled the seats next to Elizabeth and soon they all had their heads together, gossiping in noisy whispers. Every few minutes the whispering erupted into laughter as they turned to look at the boys' table.

"They're talking about Jenny's slumber party," Cristin said. "I heard about it in math class. She's inviting half the school."

"You and me?"

Cristin pulled her glasses down on her nose so that she was looking over the rims at Anna. "Dream on. Do you know what our chances are of being invited?" She made a circle with her thumb and forefinger. "Zippo."

Anna silently agreed but slumber parties were great fun. At Karen Birch's all the girls had gone outside in the dark and jumped on Karen's trampoline. Then they had sat in a circle on the mat and told ghost stories until midnight. Anna wondered what Jenny had planned for her slumber party.

"Hey Musk, seen my SuperBall?" Mark asked as he walked by, looking on the floor.

"Get lost," Cristin said.

"Turn blue." Mark pulled out a chair and knelt down, looking under the table.

Anna waited until Mark was out of sight to tell Cristin about the note in the potted plant. "And then Mrs. Moore told me that I can't be in the spelling bee because I'm not thirteen yet."

"You? The world's greatest speller?" Cristin asked. Her eyes narrowed behind her glasses. "That stinks."

"I know. Life is not fair," Anna echoed her earlier thoughts.

"My mother always says that fair has to do with the weather," Cristin said. "Want my brownie? That'll make you feel better."

Anna crinkled up her nose at the brownie with a finger hole in the top. "No thanks."

The bell rang and students began to leave.

Anna started to follow Cristin. As she stood, her feet jerked back and her tray crashed on the table. Grabbing the table to keep from falling, she barely missed going face-forward into her plate. She tried to move again but her feet yanked backwards.

From the other end of the table, Mark Pointer clapped his hands and howled with laughter. Jenny and Elizabeth and their court turned around to see what had happened—as did most of the cafeteria.

Anna looked down. Mark had tied her shoelaces to the legs of her chair.

Chapter Three

Anna scraped the cat food into the dish, turning her head and wrinkling her nose against the smell.

"Gourmet Seafood Platter Dinner." She read the can label to Risky, who rubbed against Anna's leg. "Sure sounds better than it smells."

Risky had become an outside kitty last month when the doctor discovered that Anna's little brother, Tommy, was allergic to cats. Actually, Tommy was allergic to everything with fur or feathers. That only left goldfish, snakes, hermit crabs and frogs as possible inside pets—excluding the pet rock that Anna's father had given her when Risky was banished to the backyard.

"It was the rage back in the 70's. Everybody had a pet rock," he had insisted. "You don't have to feed it, walk it or take it to the vet. It doesn't bite, chew up the furniture or chase cars."

Anna's father loved to make her laugh but the pet rock had only made her miss Risky that much more. The black cat had slept on her bed every night and Anna missed the warm lump between her feet.

As the cat ate her gourmet dinner, Anna sat on the back steps and talked to her. "In case, you're wondering, I had a rotten day at school." Risky looked up, licking her whiskers. "But there's one thing that might help me survive the rest of the year."

She had thought about it all the way home on the bus. All she had to do was convince her mother. Since she got home, Anna had vacuumed and dusted the living room and cleared Tommy's dinosaur collection from the dining table. Her mother would be impressed.

"This is my last hope," she told Risky.

An hour later, Mrs. Browning struggled into the kitchen, her face hidden by two grocery bags. Dumping the grocery bags on the counter, she slipped out of her coat and smiled at Anna.

"How's my favorite daughter?" she asked Anna.

"I'm your only daughter," Anna reminded her.

Mrs. Browning reached out and tucked a strand of Anna's blonde hair behind her ear. The affectionate gesture bugged Anna but she stood still until her mom turned around. Then Anna flipped the hair back into place. She hated for her ears to show.

Anna peeked into the bags, looking for peanut butter cookies but finding organic rice patties and celery. Her mother was on a new diet—again. The last one was hot dogs, cottage cheese and a cup of vanilla ice cream. Her mom had quickly tired of the hot dogs—after gaining three pounds. She still looked skinny to Anna.

Mrs. Browning started putting the groceries away. "Livingroom looks lovely. What's the special occasion?"

"Nothing," Anna said. "Just thought I'd try to help out more." Anna waited for her mother's reaction, knowing she must be tired after a long day. Being head counselor at Northside High School demanded lots of energy. "I also did my homework and practiced for a half an hour."

"Since you're being so industrious, how about taking out the garbage?"

"Can't Tommy take it out?" Anna asked. "I need to talk to you about something."

Her mother emptied grocery bags, putting the Cheerios in the cabinet and the eggs in the little oval slots on the refrigerator door.

"Your little brother has his jobs. Besides, Princess, you're almost thirteen. You need to accept more responsibility."

Anna dragged the garbage can from under the kitchen sink and stomped out the back door, scaring Risky. Almost thirteen. Big deal. She was still twelve and being twelve—almost thirteen—was a pain. Her little brother, who was eight years old, got away with murder while she did all the work.

Finishing the job, Anna returned to the kitchen where her mother had started dinner.

"Wash your hands," Mrs. Browning reminded her. "How was school today?"

"Just school. Usual stuff."

"I heard about the spelling bee. Your teacher called me at work. I know you're disappointed."

Anna shrugged and tried to sound responsible. "I'll try again next year."

The worse part of being disqualified had come after lunch. Anna found out that since Mark Pointer had been the first runner-up in the class, he got to take her place in the school spelling bee. That was the final blow.

"Well, look on the bright side. Since you don't have to study spelling words, maybe you'll have more time to practice your viola."

"I suppose," Anna said, rinsing her hands. She'd have lots of spare time. Especially on Monday nights when All-City was rehearsing. And during Spring Break.

Mrs. Browning handed her a towel. "I called Mrs. Sanders today and talked to her about private viola lessons for you."

Private lessons! Anna dropped the towel and stared open-mouthed at her mother. She had wished for private viola lessons last year but didn't mention them to her parents after she saw the bill for her braces.

"How do Tuesday afternoons sound?" Mrs. Browning said. "You can start next week."

Anna danced around the kitchen before giving her mom a bear hug. When Tommy walked in, she grabbed him and, without thinking, gave him a big kiss on the forehead.

"Yuk," he said, wiping the spot with the back of his hand and running from the room.

"Now, what else did you want to talk about?" Mrs. Browning asked.

Anna stopped dancing. After the private lessons, what she wanted would sound silly. She hesitated telling her mother, but it was very, very important. It could change her life.

"New tennis shoes."

"And what's wrong with the ones you are wearing?"

"They're white. Everybody is wearing colored ones. Everybody but me. I'm the only girl in the whole school in white."

With raised eyebrows, Mrs. Browning looked at Anna. "The only girl in the whole school?"

"Mom, you know what I mean."

"And how much are these wonderful shoes?"

Too much. Even if they were on sale, Anna knew they were too expensive. But she would just die if she didn't get a pair. Then when she walked down the hall, she would be like the other girls. And after gym class, maybe she could hang out with Elizabeth, Jenny and their friends, trading shoes until each girl had a different color on each foot. Nobody wanted to trade for a white shoe.

"Cristin says they're on sale at the mall for twenty-seven dollars."

Her mother nodded her head slowly. "And these shoes are very important?"

Anna nodded back, her head bobbing up and down like it was on a spring. "Very important." Maybe the most important thing in the whole world.

Opening the cabinets, her mother took out the dinner plates and handed them to Anna. "Well, I'll make a deal with you. You pay half and I'll pay half. I'll give you extra money for odd jobs around the house and you save your allowance."

Anna's hopes sank like a rock. Her allowance was only ten dollars a week and she had to pay for her lunches at school out of that. Setting the plates on the dining table, she tried to count the number of days it would take to save almost fourteen dollars. Even if she worked hard, it would take forever to get the money.

Slipping out the back door, Anna found Risky dozing on the porch steps. She scooped up the cat and nestled her cheek against the soft black fur.

"Forget the new tennis shoes," she said. She'd continue being the school's social outcast.

"Tickles died last night."

Anna looked at Cristin with suspicion. Was this a joke? Cristin's sense of humor ranged from strange to ultra sophisticated. And Anna couldn't always tell when her best friend was serious because Cristin's dimples were on display most of the time.

"Tickles?"

"My hamster, silly. She croaked." Cristin's dimples had disappeared. "I went to tell her good-night and she was stiff."

"So what did you do with her?"

"Mom made me bury her in the back yard before I came to school. I held a short funeral."

The two girls sat in orchestra class waiting for Mrs. Sanders to start the rehearsal. Anna was supposed to be practicing but she thought about the little hamster. Too bad it couldn't have been Mark Pointer.

The orchestra warmed up, the mixture of scales, exercises and music sounding like outer space music. Two students fiddled away with a hoedown, racing each other as they quickened the tempo. Mark Pointer perched on his bass stool, his string bass laying on the floor, and read the latest issue of *Trans-World Skateboard*.

Mrs. Sanders took her place on the podium. "Class, I'd like to introduce to you our newest orchestra member." She gestured to the back of the classroom. Everyone turned and stared at the dark-haired boy holding a violin. "This is Peter Edwards. Peter's moved here from California and we're very glad to have him. He's going to play the Accolay *Concerto* after school today for his All-City audition."

"Wow," Cristin whispered over the music stand to Anna. "He's cute."

Anna nodded in agreement. "Think he'll pass the audition?"

"Get serious," Cristin said. "The Accolay is major league. My brother didn't play it until he was in the tenth grade. This guy must be fantastic."

Peter took a seat in the back of the first violins but Anna saw right away that he wouldn't be there long. As the new boy tuned his instrument, the entire class seemed to be watching how well he handled the bow, playing two strings together and slightly turning the pegs until the pitches were perfect.

Cristin signaled to Anna. "Look who's starting to get very nervous." She pointed to the concertmaster of the orchestra who sat stiffly in his chair. "He's got new competition."

As the new boy warmed up, he zipped through a three-octave scale, shifting in and out of the higher positions, his fingers moving fluidly over the strings. Anna tried not to stare but she couldn't help herself. Bet he never got trapped in half position, she thought.

"Looks like a twirp to me," said Mark. He hit Anna on the arm with his bow. "You two should go steady. A twirp and a musk." He made loud kissing noises as Anna turned three shades of red.

Mrs. Sanders worked the orchestra through several scales then started rehearsing the Mozart piece, *Eine Kleine Nachtmusik* which meant "a little night music." Halfway through the first page, Anna discovered she could hear the new violinist over the rest of the orchestra. Not only was he good, he sounded like a leader.

The orchestra attacked the last section of the Mozart with energy, the dynamic level of the music growing more intense with every measure. Anna tried to match the drive of the new violinist, inspired by his powerful sound. But as she brought her bow down on the string for the last chord, a shower of white hair fell over her face, her instrument and her hand. All the hair in her bow had fallen out.

"Wow, look at Musk," Brent said, pointing at her.

She sat frozen in her chair as the orchestra laughed.

"That makes a nice wig," Mark said. "And a definite improvement over her hairdo."

Mrs. Sanders stepped down and reached over to take the bow. The hair had fallen out at the tip of the bow but was still attached at the other end.

"No problem. Just a freaky accident," the teacher said. "But you'll need to get the bow rehaired. I'll loan you a bow until you can get this one fixed."

Anna hid her red face from the class as she leaned over to put the old bow in her case. Had Peter laughed? She was too embarrassed to look. And she wanted to strangle Brent Norcross. Now the new boy probably thought her name was Musk. A freaky accident? Why did all the dumb things always happen to her?

The orchestra started playing again but Anna had lost her enthusiasm. Between pieces, Anna glanced over at Peter. He wasn't very tall but he looked nice. Nice? What did that mean? Actually, she admitted to herself, Cristin was right. He was awfully cute.

As the class began putting away their instruments, Mrs. Sanders called Anna to the front of the room. "Don't worry about the bow. It wasn't your fault."

Sure, Anna thought, I just happen to be in the wrong place at the wrong time—every day of my entire life.

"I notice that Mark's still pestering you."

"Not really," Anna said, crossing her fingers to cover the lie.

Mrs. Sanders smiled and patted Anna on the shoulder. "Come by after school for a minute and we'll talk about my newest idea. I've got a plan that should stop Mark from bothering you."

As Anna made her way to social studies class, her mind felt like a whirlwind. The new boy would be in the orchestra room after school. And she could hardly wait for school to be out so she could hear Mrs. Sanders' plan.

Could anything get rid of Mark Pointer?

CHAPTER FOUR ||

"Number nineteen is a preposition. And number twenty is a direct object," Miss Moore, the language arts teacher, said as the class checked their homework assignments.

Anna looked out the window and wondered what color tennis shoes she should buy—if she ever saved enough money. Elizabeth Jenkins had two pair, blue and lavender. Plus enough sweaters to outfit the entire seventh grade. And Jenny Arrington had a pink pair that matched every outfit she wore. All of Jenny's clothes were pink, even her underwear. The girl was batty about the color pink.

"Number twenty-six has two answers. I'll give extra credit if you get both correct . . . ."

Anna glanced at her paper, then out the window at the group of people who waited across the street for the city bus.

If she had had her shoes that morning Jenny and Elizabeth might have asked her to trade with them after gym class. Instead Anna had watched as they swapped shoes with the other girls until their feet looked like a traveling rainbow when they walked down the hall.

"Pass your papers to the front of each row." The teacher collected the papers and stretched a rubber band around them. "Now, I've got some exciting news. As you remember, Mark Pointer represented our class in the spelling bee. This morning he won first place in the school, outspelling the eighth and ninth graders."

Several of the boys clapped their hands loudly. "'Way to go, Marko baby."

"Thank you, no autographs, please," Mark said, standing and taking a bow.

Anna didn't laugh. The only thing Mark should have won was the prize as the biggest pain in the school. That would be no contest.

"We're going to help Mark win the trophy for the entire school district," the teacher continued. "We need a coach who will read the words to him so he can practice spelling. We need someone who's dependable and also a good speller. Are there any volunteers?"

The class got quiet very quickly.

No one in their right mind would volunteer for that job, Anna thought. It would be like inviting a vampire into your home to spend the night.

"Anna?" the teacher said. "Several teachers have suggested that you be Mark's coach. I know you won't let us down."

Anna's mouth hung open as if she were taking a dose of medicine. Had she heard the teacher right? No sound came from her throat as she frantically tried to tell the teacher that she couldn't be Mark's coach. Not in a million, trillion years. But all that came out were strange squeaking noises.

"Give me a break," Mark moaned. "At least find someone who can speak English and not mouseketeer."

The teacher frowned at him as the class laughed. "May I remind you, Mr. Pointer, that if Anna was thirteen she would be competing against you. Remember, she's already won the district championship twice. Be thankful that she's your coach and not in the contest."

Within Anna's panic, she heard the word 'thirteen.' How many problems would be solved by that magic number? If she were thirteen, she'd show nasty Mark Pointer how to spell, on stage, in front of the judges, by beating the socks off him. Maybe her mother had miscounted her birthdays. Maybe there was a hidden birth certificate that proved she was a year older. Maybe she'd catch the Black Plague and not have to coach Mark.

When the class left for lunch, Anna lingered at the teacher's desk.

"I can't coach Mark," she blurted. The words tumbled out so fast they ran over each other. "I've got to practice, I've got private lessons now, tons of homework, and I have to do all the housework at home, plus take out the garbage."

She didn't mean to say that she did all the housework. It popped out of her mouth with no warning.

"You're my best speller," the teacher said.

"But I'm not thirteen," Anna said. She was grasping at any reason not to be Mark's coach.

"Maybe this is a little unfair since you were disqualified."

Anna nodded her head so hard that it made her dizzy.

"But think about how all the practice will help you next year." The teacher grinned. "You'll probably win easily."

"What about my homework?" Anna asked. "And my practicing?"

The teacher pursed her lips and tapped her pencil on the desk. "I'll make you a deal. I'll postpone your book reports until after the spelling bee. That'll give you extra time. All I'm asking for is thirty minutes every afternoon. You don't have any other special projects due now, do you?"

"No ma'am." Anna sighed. Nothing special in her life at all.

"Wonderful. You're such a responsible student. I knew we could depend on you."

Responsible. There was that word again. The reward for being responsible was spending thirty minutes every day with Mark Pointer. Thirty minutes in a torture chamber. How many horrible things could he do to her during a half-hour?

"This is your last chance," Cristin said. "Are you coming with me or not?"

Anna walked down the hall with her head down as she carefully stepped in the middle of each floor tile. Maybe if she didn't step on a crack, some form of good luck would change her fate. Maybe if she didn't miss a tile all the way to the orchestra room . . . .

"Earth to Anna." Cristin snapped her fingers in front of her friend's nose.

"Coming where?" Anna said, without missing a step.

"My mom's waiting to take us to the mall to buy me a new hamster. I invited you yesterday. Are you listening?"

Anna stopped, careful to keep her white tennis shoes within the tiles, and faced Cristin. "I was picked to coach Mark Pointer for the spelling bee."

Cristin's eyes grew to saucer size behind her glasses and she gasped, one hand covering her mouth. "No way, I'd commit hara-kiri first. Tell the teacher you can't." Her voice grew louder. "Get your mother to write a note. Leave the country. Don't just stand there, you nitwit, do something."

"I can't get out of it and I can't go to the mall," Anna said, shaking her head. "Mrs. Sanders said for me to come by the orchestra room after school today." She hesitated telling Cristin what Mrs. Sanders had promised. Could the orchestra director rescue her from the torture ahead?

When she reached the orchestra room, she slipped into a chair near the door. The new boy was warming up, playing scales and arpeggios, his head bent over his violin in concentration.

Sitting in a chair near the piano, Dr. Giacomo, the conductor of the All-City Orchestra seemed to be absorbed in the stack of music on his lap. Anna recognized him after having seen his picture in the newspaper several times. With his reading glasses perched on his nose, he looked very stern. Cristin had once told Anna that he sometimes yelled at the kids if they didn't play their best.

Mrs. Sanders sat at the piano, practicing the accompaniment to the concerto. "Ready, Peter?" she asked.

He nodded and walked over to the piano. Blowing on his left hand, he told Mrs. Sanders, "My hands always sweat when I have to play a solo."

The teacher looked over at Anna and winked. "Lots of people have that problem."

Peter began playing the concerto. The opening notes were graceful and smooth, the complicated rhythms exciting. He made the music soar like an eagle, then, moments later, whisper like the wind. Anna listened without moving, not noticing when the custodian barged in to empty the trashcans.

She wanted to be able to play like that. The nimble fingers. The graceful bow arm. The velvet sound. She would practice twelve hours a day. Whatever it took, she would do it.

The custodian stood in the middle of the room, grinning and clutching the trash can to his chest. "Boy, you sure can make that fiddle talk. Can you play a hoedown?"

The new boy looked to Mrs. Sanders for help.

"Not yet," she said. "But I'll teach him the *Orange Blossom Special* and we'll give you a private concert."

As the custodian left he muttered and tsk-tsked about Peter's flying fingers. Anna silently agreed with him but stayed in her chair as Peter wiped the layer of rosin from his strings and loosened his bow.

"Very nice performance, Peter," the conductor said, standing and shaking Peter's hand. "I've signed your application for All-City. Your first rehearsal is next Monday evening at the high school. We're delighted to have you."

After the conductor left, Anna wanted to say something to Peter, something about how well he played and something about how much she admired him. But she pressed her lips together, afraid she'd say something stupid. She had already been laughed at twice that day.

Peter finished latching his case and picked up his music. "Have you already auditioned?" he asked Anna.

"No," she said, "I mean I want to—but not yet." Her face began to burn with embarrassment. She sounded like a dimwit.

"Anna will be auditioning next fall," said Mrs. Sanders. "She's one of our best violists."

Peter nodded. "I hope you make it." Then he grinned. He had a cocky grin that Anna liked. "And I hope you get your bow fixed. That happened to me once."

Somehow Anna got her tongue to working again. "You were terrific—I mean your audition was terrific."

"Thanks. See you tomorrow in orchestra."

Anna could feel her heart pounding as he walked out the door. And her hands were sweaty. Maybe tomorrow she'd think up something brilliant to say to him. Maybe she'd tell him that they had a lot in common, sweaty hands and freaky bows.

Maybe tomorrow they could have a real conversation.

Motioning for Anna to join her, Mrs. Sanders pulled two chairs from the orchestra set. "Now, let's talk about Mark. I spoke with your guidance counselor and we've come up with a plan of action."

Anna leaned forward so she wouldn't miss a word. This was going to save her from a fate worse than death.

"I want you to ignore him."

Ignore Mark Pointer? Was this some kind of a joke? Could you ignore Godzilla?

"You see, Anna, he wants attention. He has to have an audience and he wants some kind of a reaction from you. You reward him when you respond."

Anna frowned. This was not the solution to her problem.

The teacher watched her carefully. "I can see by the look on your face that you don't believe me. Think for a moment. What do you do when Mark pesters you?"

The answer was easy. She died a thousand deaths.

Mrs. Sanders answered for her. "You respond in some way. Now I want you to ignore him. Pretend that he's invisible. Act like you didn't hear what he said. Think you can handle that?"

Anna's heart sank to the bottom of her stomach. Mrs. Sanders had been her last hope. She was doomed now. How was she supposed to ignore Mark and call out his spelling words? It would never work. Never.

"Try it for a week and we'll see what happens."

A week? She had to face Mark the Monster tomorrow afternoon.

CHAPTER FIVE

Ringing the bell once, Anna stepped back from the front door, hoping no one would hear it. Somewhere within the house a dog barked. Then she heard footsteps and a pretty lady opened the front door.

"Anna, I recognize you from the fall concert," the lady said, smiling. "Please come in."

Anna followed her into the living room and perched on the edge of a blue couch. As she looked around the room, she folded her hands in her lap and cleared her throat. Matching blue curtains framed the bay window and an Oriental rug covered the floor. Next to Anna, on an end table, was a picture of a little boy dressed in a sailor suit, holding a toy boat. She knew in an instant who it was.

As the lady sat down across from Anna, a flying bundle of beige fur hurled itself into Anna's lap and began licking her face.

"Boots," the lady scolded, "get down right now." She leaned over and nudged the little dog from Anna's lap. The dog's bright button eyes were almost hidden by its curly, cream-colored hair. Boots scampered in a circle around the room then leaped back into Anna's arms.

"Boots is supposed to be our watch dog. But he'd probably lick a burglar to death." The lady laughed, her long brown hair brushing her shoulders. How could such a pretty woman be Mark Pointer's mother? Anna had half-expected someone with fangs and red eyes. Boots stiffened and cocked his head before springing through the air again when Mark walked into the room.

Pushing the dog away, Mark fell into an armchair, one leg dangling over an arm and the other tucked under him. He didn't say "hello Musk" or "drop dead" or "get out of my face." Nothing.

Mrs. Pointer stood to one side and looked at her son. She never spoke but raised one eyebrow. Quickly Mark sat up and put his feet on the floor.

"I know you two have work to do, so I'll leave and take Boots with me," Mrs. Pointer said.

When she left the room, Mark scowled at Anna but didn't say anything for a minute. Finally, he handed Anna the list of spelling words. "Here. Start on the third set. I know all the first two sets perfectly."

Anna sat very still on the couch. Being alone in the room with Mark felt eerie. Would he try something? Without an audience? She looked down at the list and giggled when she read the first word.

"What's so funny?" Mark demanded.

"Nothing."

"So call out the words."

"First word. Annihilate," she said, trying hard not to laugh. She knew the meaning of the word. Annihilate: to reduce to nothing. Annihilate Mark Pointer. Great idea. That would be much more effective than ignoring him.

They worked as Anna called out the words and he spelled. If he missed one, she marked it on the list so he could study the word later. Mark said nothing to her, just sat in the chair and spelled.

They were almost through when a tall teen-age girl with long brown hair slammed through the front door. She seemed not to notice Anna and Mark as she tossed her books on an empty chair.

In her designer jeans and cool T-shirt, she was the most beautiful teen-ager Anna had ever seen.

"Do you know what he did this time?" she shouted as she disappeared into another room. "He was late picking me up at school, then made me loan him money so he could buy me a chocolate shake. Now explain that to me."

Anna listened with fascination. The girl must have a boyfriend. Anna wondered what it would be like to have a boy pick you up after school. Maybe someone like Peter who was talented and cute.

"And then he says we have to go to her house on Saturday," the girl continued. "I hate her and I hate her bratty kids."

Anna noticed that Mark hadn't spelled the last word she had called out. "Sculpture," she repeated. But Mark stared at the floor, his lips pinched together.

"Keep your voice down, Dana," Mrs. Pointer said.

"Mom, I'm not going. And that's final. He can take Mark with him but I'm staying home."

Anna heard Mark swallow hard. Was Mark going somewhere with his sister's boyfriend? Did little brothers go on dates with older sisters? If so, Anna was never going out with a boy. Her little brother was the world's champion tattle.

Before Anna could call out 'sculpture' for the third time, Mrs. Pointer walked into the room with a plate of brownies.

"All that work probably made you hungry."

"We're through," Mark said, glaring at Anna. "And Anna has to go home."

Quickly gathering her books, she got the message. "I have to do my homework and then practice."

"Well, take a couple of brownies with you so you'll have lots of energy. I wish Mark would practice without having to be told." She smiled and Anna thought again that she was as beautiful as her daughter. "Mark, show your guest to the door. And tell her thank you for helping you."

Anna took a brownie and escaped. Mark acted so weird. He didn't make fun of her. He didn't make embarrassing noises. He didn't call her 'Musk.' He had even mumbled something that sounded like thanks as she left. And he didn't even try to shut the door on her foot like he did last week in the school cafeteria. Maybe he was saving something for tomorrow in orchestra.

Whatever was wrong with Mark made Anna walk faster as she headed home, eating the brownie.

The following afternoons were like slow-motion replays of the first. Anna sat in the living room with Mark and called out spelling words. Mark answered like a robot. Hemoglobin . . . calligraphy . . . fluoride. The lists seemed to go on forever. Anna did admit to herself that Mark was a good speller. Maybe great. He rarely missed more than two words from each group of forty. And the next day he could always spell the ones he missed.

Every afternoon Boots jumped in her lap to be petted and Mrs. Pointer produced more brownies or oatmeal cookies when they finished. And his mother always reminded Mark to say thank you to Anna as she left.

Tuesday, and Anna's first private lesson, seemed to take forever to arrive. She stood in the music room of Mrs. Sanders' home thinking that it was easy to tell that musicians lived in the house. The room seemed to be crammed with music, instruments, records, stereo equipment and books about music. A grand piano stood in one corner of the room and a harpsichord across from it. Anna lightly touched the keys of the harpsichord, fascinated with its tinkling, unique sound.

"Like the harpsichord?" Mrs. Sanders asked. "My husband built it from a kit."

"It's neat." As Anna pushed the keys, she could see the quill mechanism pluck the strings. Maybe next year she'd take piano lessons, she decided.

"Let's get started," Mrs. Sanders said. She opened the new scale book on the music stand. "It's important to warm up the fingers and the brain with scales before you work on exercises or pieces."

Playing the scale, Anna concentrated on Mrs. Sanders' instructions. Longer bow strokes . . . keep the bow straight . . . faster bow. Soon she could hear the improvement in her tone. The sound grew clearer and richer. Her goal was to sound like Peter Edwards.

More new music, an exercise book and a student concerto appeared on the music stand. Anna sight-read the concerto, careful to follow the bowings and making sure her fingers pressed down on the strings in the correct patterns. Mrs. Sanders said that there would be a recital in the spring and Anna would perform a solo.

Too soon, the lesson was over. Mrs. Sanders' cat, Yo-yo, rubbed against her leg as Anna reluctantly put her viola away. She wished the lesson could have lasted an hour and that she could stay and play the harpsichord.

"When will your bow be ready?" Mrs. Sanders asked.

"Maybe by the end of the week. My Dad's going to call."

Mrs. Sanders smiled slowly. "Good. That's perfect timing. I was watching you play the Brandenburg in orchestra today. Still having half position problems?"

Anna picked up her new music from the music stand, nodding her head. Even with the teacher's help, she was still trapped in half position.

"I'd like to make a deal with you," said Mrs. Sanders. "If you can play the half position section of the Brandenburg perfectly, two weeks from today, I'll let that be your audition for All-City Youth Orchestra."

Had Anna imagined what Mrs. Sanders had said? An audition for All-City? "B-b-but I'm not thirteen yet."

"I know. But I spoke to the conductor and if you can conquer half position, we'll make an exception in your case."

Anna could hardly contain her excitement. "I'll work very hard. And I'll practice twelve hours a day. I promise." She'd skip meals.

She'd do without sleep. Maybe her mother would excuse her from taking out the garbage. Nothing could stand in her way. Not now.

Then she remembered the half position. Could she pass the audition?

CHAPTER SIX ‖

For Friday's lunch, the printed menu on the main bulletin board had boasted of "mystery" meat, lima beans, fruit medley, celery "boats" and fries. Anna stared down at her lunch. The "mystery" meat resembled the food her uncle fed his rabbits and the celery "boats" looked like they had been bombed.

Across the cafeteria Mark Pointer blew the paper wrapper off his straw, hitting an eighth grader on the back of the head. When the kid turned around to see what the commotion was about, Brent and Mark laughed and pointed at him. Soon the entire table was blowing straw wrappers and the teachers came running.

"He's such a child," Cristin said, watching them clean up the mess.

Anna nodded. Yesterday he had thrown her science book into the boys' restroom and dared her to go get it. She begged him to please go get her book but he just stood in the middle of the hall and laughed. Then she tried to bribe him with candy. Five jawbreakers and a pack of bubble gum. But he took the candy and walked away.

"He's the only drawback to being in All-City," Cristin said. "Now you'll have to put up with him at school, after school and on Monday nights."

Anna didn't care. Being in All-City was worth walking over burning coals. Mark Pointer couldn't stop her.

"What do you call someone who can be two different people?" Anna asked Cristin.

"Two-faced."

"No. I mean different personalities."

If Anna could figure out what made Mark act almost nice at his house, maybe she could get him to act that way at school. And, if she passed the audition, at All-City.

Cristin thought for a moment. "I give up. What do they call them?"

Before she could answer, Mark walked up to their table. Instinctively, Anna scooted her chair back as if to protect herself. Cristin, using her two index fingers, made the sign of a cross as if to ward off a vampire.

"Back, back, you evil monster," Cristin said, pretending to be scared.

Mark sneered at her. "Takes one to know one, four eyes." Then he turned to Anna. "Don't bother coming to my house today," he said. "My dad's picking me up after school."

"Picking you up?" Cristin asked. "Isn't that what they do to garbage?"

Anna tried to smother a laugh with her hand. She wished that she could talk back to Mark like Cristin. Maybe that was why Mark never picked on her best friend.

Mark edged closer to the table. "You think you're so funny. If you have to know, smarty, my dad's taking me to the music store to buy me an electric bass guitar. And an amplifier. And Mrs. Sanders is going to teach me how to play it so I can join a rock band."

"Big deal."

He glared at Cristin. "When I'm rich and famous, you'll be sorry. You'll have to pay a lot of money to hear me play." He put his hands on his hips. "I won't even give you an autograph."

Cristin pretended to clutch at her heart. "My heart is broken. My life is ruined."

"Very funny," Mark said. He turned and walked away.

"We won't hold our breath," Anna said in a rush of courage. But Mark was gone. She giggled. Even if he hadn't heard her, it felt good to know she had tried.

"I'm so excited about your audition," Cristin said. "Promise me that you're practicing?"

Anna nodded. She spent almost an hour a day practicing—twenty minutes on the half position. But she still couldn't shift back.

"Then there's nothing to worry about. You'll be fantastic." Cristin's dimples grew deeper. "We're going to Disney World and be roommates and sit on the bus together. I can't wait for Spring Break."

Anna wished she could share Cristin's enthusiasm. If only she could shift in and out of half position one time, she'd feel like she was making progress.

"I just don't understand why you're having so much trouble," Cristin said as if she could read Anna's mind. "Half position is a piece of cake. You slide your hand backwards a half an inch and back again." Cristin measured the movement in the air with her left hand. "There are a trillion other things in music that are hard—like third position or vibrato."

Cristin was right. However, for some quirky reason, Anna couldn't get the motion right. Somehow, she had to get out of half position and into All-City Orchestra.

"Here," the girl sitting next to Anna said. She thrust several envelopes into Anna's hand. "Pass them down."

Anna held the envelopes over her tray so that none of the "mystery meat" would get on them. The tiny envelopes were pink and were addressed in dark pink ink. Pink butterfly stickers sealed the flaps closed.

"Invitations to Jenny's slumber party," she told Cristin.

Anna flipped through the envelopes, reading the names.

"Well?" Cristin asked.

Anna shook her head and passed them down the table to the other girls. "Maybe she hasn't given all of them out yet."

The two girls looked down the table to where Jenny and Elizabeth reigned. Four other girls surrounded them, hanging on to every word they said, laughing when Elizabeth or Jenny laughed and copying all Jenny and Elizabeth's movements.

"It's no big deal," Cristin said.

But it was to Anna. She decided that she had to do something to get Jenny's attention. She had to do something that would make Jenny want to invite her to the slumber party.

Anna mentally counted up the money her mom owed her for allowance and extra jobs. She had swept the garage, dusted the furniture, washed the dishes twice and vacuumed, and she had skipped lunch three times. Since Friday was payday, Anna might have enough money for her new tennis shoes.

When Anna got off the school bus, a strange truck was parked in her driveway and a man in overalls knelt in the front yard, cutting metal pipes.

Inside the house, a lake stood where the kitchen floor used to be. Barefooted, with her jeans rolled up to the knees, Mrs. Browning swept water in long waves out the back door.

"Grab a mop, Anna and start working. The water heater burst. Thank goodness I was home when it happened. Otherwise, the carpet would have been ruined."

Anna's little brother, Tommy, slipped across the floor, sending water over Anna's feet.

"Tommy, get out," commanded their mother. "Go to your room and stay there until I call you."

Why did he miss all the work, Anna thought as she mopped. Because he's the baby and I have to be responsible. She had heard it so many times that she had memorized her mother's speech. "You're twelve, and that means you're no longer a child." And, like the Language Arts teacher said, Anna was responsible. She hated being twelve and, most of all, being responsible.

Mrs. Browning and Anna were still mopping the kitchen floor when Anna's father arrived. "Four hundred and sixty-four dollars?" he asked looking at the plumber's bill. "Is it made out of gold?"

"And perfect timing. Today was payday," Mrs. Browning added.

Mr. Browning put his arm around Anna's shoulder. "Well, at least we've got some good-looking help here."

Anna made a funny face at him and he tweaked her nose. Her dad always found something to laugh about, even a monster-sized plumbing bill.

"Thanks for your help, Princess," her mother said. "I hate to tell you but I can't pay you for the extra jobs now. The bill wiped me out. Can you wait until next week?"

Another week? Anna's heart plunged. So much for Jenny's slumber party. Without the new shoes, they'd never invite her. But she understood—or least she tried to understand. She was, as usual, responsible.

That night, Anna practiced for over an hour. She followed Mrs. Sanders' directions and took out each measure of the half position and played it slowly. Over and over, she worked to move her hand smoothly, without stopping or jerking, until she could glide back to first position. But she stayed trapped in half position as if her hand were glued there. If she stopped, she could move her hand back into place. But that would never get her into All-City.

She finally managed to play the measure right once. But the audition was less than two weeks away. Would she make it? Anna carefully put her viola back in the case and plopped down on the bed, hugging Pooh bear to her chest.

No new shoes. She didn't even bother to ask. Now Jenny and Elizabeth would never invite her anywhere. Or ask her to sit with them after gym class. Or pass notes with her.

She snuggled deeper into her collection of stuffed animals, fluffing the ears on the bunnies and retying the bows on the bears. Her favorite was Pooh bear whom Anna had had since she was a baby. The felt "honey" pot that he used to clutch in his fat arms was missing, along with the gold buttons on his red jacket. But who noticed.

If only she could play the Bach. And if only she didn't have to coach Mark Pointer. And if only she had a pair of colored tennis shoes. She kicked at one white tennis shoe and tried to imagine it as blue. Or red. Or orange. She had never decided what color she wanted. Wonder what color would look best?

In the right-hand drawer of her desk lay a new pack of Magic Markers left over from the poster project for science class. She uncapped the blue marker and drew a blue sunset on the toe of her shoes. Then she tried yellow. Two squares on each heel. And red stripes between the laces. Purple scallops around the edge of the sole. Before she realized it, both shoes looked like the inside of a kaleidoscope.

Boy, was she going to be in trouble when her mom saw the shoes.

CHAPTER SEVEN ‖

The orchestra sat quietly, instruments in rest position as Mrs. Sanders went down the roll. The playing test consisted of a G Major scale and the dreaded half position passage from the *Brandenburg*. Yesterday the violins had been tested and today the violas, cellos and string bass had to play.

"Relax and quit biting your lip," Cristin whispered to Anna. "You can do it."

But that was easy for her to say, Cristin had already played. And if Anna's ears were operating properly, Cristin had probably made an easy A. Anna rubbed her sweaty hands on her jeans but the water continued to pour from her skin as if someone had turned on a faucet. The lifelines in her palms glistened like miniature rivers.

"Anna, you're next," the teacher said.

Brent turned around and whispered, "Prepare to be humiliated." The cellist beside him snickered.

Trying to ignore them, Anna waited for one of Mark's prize cutdowns. But he sat on his stool, reading the *Rock Scene* magazine he kept hidden in his orchestra folder. Brent started to add another comment but looked at Mark, then shut his mouth.

Mrs. Sanders finished writing in her grade book." The G Major scale first, please."

The scale was a cinch. Anna had practiced it every day. The first eight notes came out well but as she tried to play on the upper strings, the slippery fingers threatened to sabotage her performance. Concentrate, she told herself. Note by note, she played, reminding herself to listen carefully.

"Very nice," Mrs. Sanders said. "Your tone is improving. How about the Bach?"

The Bach. The half position. The Trap. Taking a deep breath, Anna looked over the music before putting the viola under her chin and placing the bow on the strings. She sailed through the beginning of the section and shifted smoothly into half position. A few of the notes sounded slightly out of tune but she pushed on. Two measures ahead . . . one measure . . . time to shift. But her hand refused to budge as if locked in place. She stopped, moved her hand back to first position then finished the passage.

"Better. Much better," the director said. "Keep up the good work. It'll come." Then she went on to test the cellos.

Tears stung Anna's eyes as she fought to keep from crying. She'd never be able to play the passage. Eight hours of practice. One hour every day. And, in spite of Mrs. Sanders' help, it had not improved one bit. To pass the audition for All-City Orchestra, she would have to be able to shift out of half position as smoothly as she got into it.

Her dream of playing in All-City vanished. If she couldn't pass the playing test at school, she couldn't pass the audition. They would play the Christmas concert without Anna. They would get their new uniforms. They would go to Disney World. Without Anna.

Depression settled around her like a fog. Maybe she should quit playing the viola. She could tell her parents to sell her instrument. And she'd get her schedule changed. She could take home economics and learn to make a skirt. Or industrial arts and make a paper towel holder.

Anna bit at her bottom lip as she listened to the next student play. Making music was special to Anna. She loved the excitement, the warm tingle inside that came from performing with the other students. How could she think, even for a moment, about quitting? Chin high, she resolved to practice harder. Maybe a week wasn't long enough.

The playing test continued through the cello section. Brent had to start his scale over three times. And his Bach sounded like a train wreck.

"Let me play again," Brent begged. "I can do better."

But Mrs. Sanders shook her head and warned that if he didn't practice more he would not perform on the Thanksgiving assembly program.

"The score is," Cristin said under her breath to Anna, "Bach seven, Brent zippo."

"But I played it perfectly at home last night," Brent said.

Cristin turned and smiled at the chubby cellist. "That must have been a neat trick since you haven't taken your cello home since last week."

Even Mrs. Sanders laughed at Brent who still insisted that he had practiced.

After the testing was finished, the class mobbed around the director's podium to get a look at their grades. Mrs. Sanders always left her grade book open after every test so that the students could see what they had made. Anna hung back, a little curious, but not really wanting to see the damage.

The new boy, Peter, waited beside Anna. "Nice playing on the test. I heard that you're going to audition for All-City next week. Hope you make it."

Anna's tongue stuck to the top of her mouth. Was he actually talking to her? In public?

"I used to have the same problem with my shifting," he continued, "when I lived in Colorado. Except I couldn't play the notes in tune—I always played flat."

"Colorado?" she said, her voice squeaking. "I thought you came from California."

"I did. I've lived almost everywhere. My dad's a colonel in the Marines."

All Anna could do was nod her head. She didn't want to squeak any more than necessary. She'd die if Peter laughed at her.

Taking her turn to look in the gradebook, she was surprised to see an eighty-seven penciled in the square next to her name. Mrs. Sanders must have been in a generous mood. Between the passing grade and talking to Peter, Anna felt like her world had started revolving again.

Back in her seat, Anna held the viola in her lap and ran her fingers across the varnished wood, lightly strumming the strings. The vibrations tickled her hand. Positioning her fingers on the strings, she pressed them to the fingerboard until the tips of her fingers were marked with straight indentions where the strings had been. She'd work harder.

Somehow she'd get the shifting correct. She knew she could do it.

"You'll never believe what happened." Cristin's big eyes peaked over the edge of the music stand. "You remember my aunt who was here from Miami?"

Anna nodded. "You mean the one who wore the dress with purple orchids?"

"Yeah. She went home yesterday. On the plane. And Whiskers stowed away in her tote bag. Somewhere over Orlando, Florida, he chewed his way out of the bag and escaped. And the flight attendant had to capture him in a barf bag."

"Whiskers?"

"My new hamster. Actually, my ex-hamster. Honestly, Anna, I don't think you ever listen to a thing I say."

First Tickles, now Whiskers. Anna laughed. The hamster must have created quite a madhouse on the plane. She could imagine the plane doing loops while everyone scrambled to catch the hamster. And Cristin's aunt standing in her seat, the dress with purple orchids pulled up above her knees.

"Hey Musk, loan me a pencil," Mark said, nudging her. "Hurry before the bell rings."

"Me too," Brent said.

Anna unzipped her purse and began digging for two pencils. Something grainy surrounded her fingers and when she withdrew her hand, her fingers had turned grayish-black.

Brent laughed so hard that he almost fell out of his chair. And Mark bent over double, cackling and slapping his knee.

Mark had emptied the pencil sharpener in her purse when she went to look at her grade. The bottom of the purse was two inches deep in pencil shavings that clung to her assignment book, hairbrush and new pack of chewing gum. The once-white insides of her purse were now streaked with gray. The purse looked like the bottom of Cristin's hamster's cage.

"Mark Pointer," she cried. "I'm going to tell—"

"Tell who? Your boyfriend Peter? Will he beat me up?" Mark asked in a loud voice.

Anna turned around quickly to hide her red face. Had Peter heard?

"Yucko, what happened to your shoes?" Mark backed away as if she had a disease. "That's the dumbest pair of shoes I've ever seen."

Anna looked down at her shoes. Covered with all the Magic Marker colors she owned, the shoes resembled Sunday's funny papers minus the words.

Brent agreed with Mark. "Musk, you are a real weirdo."

Luckily, the bell rang before they could tell the entire orchestra. As the orchestra students filed out the door, she still looked down at her feet.

Brent's right, Anna thought, I am weird.

When Mrs. Pointer answered the door, Anna pinched her lips closed to keep from blurting out what Mark had done to her at school that day. Did Mrs. Pointer know that she lived with a horrible, two-faced monster? Instead, Anna walked in, sat down on the couch and waited for Mark.

"He'll be here in a second. He's finishing his homework," Mrs. Pointer said. "How was school today?"

"Fine," Anna lied.

"Is your father going to coach the baseball team this spring?"

Anna shrugged. "I'm not sure." Her father was always doing something with the kids. Her mother called him the neighborhood Pied Piper.

"Mark enjoyed playing on his team last year. I thought he was an excellent coach. Lots of patience with the boys. And a great sense of humor. Is he always that funny at home?"

"He thinks he is," Anna said.

Mrs. Pointer smiled and Anna wondered again how Mark could have such a pretty mother. Maybe he was adopted. Or maybe his parents found him in an alley and felt sorry for him. But then who would want someone as rotten as Mark? Anna decided that he must take after his father.

Boots sniffed his way into the room and, seeing Anna, jumped in her lap. As she petted the little dog, she glanced over at the picture of Mark on the end table, wishing she had her Magic Markers. Fangs hanging from his mouth and horns protruding from his hair would complete his real image.

Mark appeared, no fangs or horns visible, and they went straight to work without any mention of Anna's purse or shoes.

From the list, Anna picked the hardest words she could find. Hemoglobin. Catastrophe. Larynx. But he spelled every word correctly. He didn't even have to ask for a definition or clarification.

Anna was impressed. She tried words from the advanced list. Hemispherical. Nitroglycerin. Bibliophile. Mark didn't miss a single one.

"Very good," she said, forgetting she was mad at him.

"Yeah, I know."

From the back of the house Mrs. Pointer cleared her throat loudly. Twice.

"Thanks," he mumbled.

"Did you get your new electric bass guitar?" Anna asked.

One eyebrow shot up and Mark glared at her, his eyes narrowing. "What's it to you?"

"Just thought I'd ask." Anna knew she was in trouble and prepared herself for one of Mark's attacks.

"Well, mind your own beeswax."

Mrs. Pointer cleared her throat again. Very loudly.

CHAPTER EIGHT

Driving to the violin shop, Mr. Browning sang along with the radio. When he stopped for a red light, he slapped his hands on the steering wheel in rhythm with the music and nodded his head with the beat. A man in the car next to them stared at Mr. Browning.

"Dad," Anna said, slipping down in her seat. "You're attracting an audience." Going anywhere with her father was unpredictable. She never knew what he was going to do. Or say. But she wouldn't trade him for a million dollars. Even with his zany sense of humor, she adored him.

"Come on, Princess," he said. "Give me a smile. I thought you liked the Beach Boys."

The light changed and Mr. Browning pulled away, singing about surfing and beach buggies.

When they arrived at the shop, Anna prayed that her father wouldn't try to be funny. Or act weird. Going to the violin shop was always special to her and she'd die if he embarrassed her.

As Anna and her father opened the door to Richter's Violin Shop, a bell jangled. Dozens of violins and violas hung from a wire that stretched the length of the shop. Some had no strings or bridges. Some were missing chinrests. A string bass stood in one corner and cellos were lined up against the wall on a rack.

Stooping down, Anna peered into the glass counter at the mutes, amber rosin and pitchpipes displayed on a velvet cloth. On the second shelf sat chinrests made of ebony and rosewood. The shop smelled of wood and varnish.

"Be with you in a moment," said the silver-haired man who was hunched over a table in the back of the shop.

Anna strolled around the room, looking at the autographed pictures of violinists who had visited the shop. Hanging on the wall was a poster of the All-City Youth Orchestra, advertising next month's Christmas concert. She searched the picture for Cristin but couldn't find her because she sat in the back—right in front of the trumpets. But no one could miss Mark and the silly grin on his face. Or the conductor, wearing a tuxedo and holding a slim baton as he stood on the podium in front of the orchestra. The conductor wasn't smiling. Anna wondered if he ever did.

She closed her eyes and imagined herself in the picture. Wearing the new uniform. Holding her instrument in rest position while the photographer took the picture. The Christmas program was five weeks away and she dreamed of being on stage, playing *Sleigh Ride* and *Little Drummer Boy* with the rest of the orchestra.

A heavy German accent interrupted her dream. "Anna, how's my favorite violist today?"

"Fine, Mr. Richter," she said to the repairman. "Is my bow ready?"

He presented the bow to her. "Here it is. New horsehair. New plug in the tip." Mr. Richter winked at Anna. "Good as new."

She turned the bow over, careful not to touch the new horsehair. Having her bow back would help a lot. Maybe that was the reason she hadn't played well that morning in class.

"Think that'll get you through the audition?" her father asked.

Mr. Richter's bushy eyebrows shot up. "She's auditioning for the youth orchestra?"

Mr. Browning nodded. "Next week. She's got it made in the shade." He beamed at Anna. "I've already bought our family's tickets for the concert."

Anna cringed at her father's comment—not because of his silly saying—but because she knew that she might not pass the audition. He didn't know that she still couldn't play the half position section. What would he say if she didn't make it? Then he'd need an extra ticket for her—to sit in the audience.

Shaking his finger at Anna, Mr. Richer said, "Practice very hard. The conductor is not easy to please. He's very demanding. Every note must be perfect. Every bow stroke exactly right."

Demanding? It was bad enough that she hadn't played well in class that morning but now Mr. Richter was warning her about the conductor. Would he yell at her at the audition? Her shoulders slumped as she left the shop. Between coaching Mark and trying to get out of half position in order to pass the audition, she already felt battered and bruised.

As she and her father left the violin shop, Anna could see the picture of the orchestra through the shop window. Did she have the courage to play for such a mean-looking conductor?

Eleven girls clustered around the mirror in the girls' locker room, each trying to repair the damage that the basketball game had done to hair and make-up. Jenny, dressed in a pink jumper and pink plaid blouse, had stopped applying her eye shadow and was whispering to Elizabeth. The four girls who usually followed Jenny and Elizabeth quit brushing their hair and looked Anna's way.

Cristin whispered in Anna's ear, "Why are Elizabeth and her shadows staring at us?"

Anna peeked behind Cristin. The other girls looked back, hairbrushes suspended in mid-air, necks craned as if they were mannequins on display in a store window.

Anna checked to see if she was fully dressed. Jeans zipped. Blouse buttoned. Hair over her ears. She wasn't allowed to wear make-up so there were no smudges to worry about. But Jenny and Elizabeth continued to stare, making Anna very nervous.

"Act normal," Cristin said, her eyes as big as basketballs. "The school's biggest snob is coming our way."

Elizabeth walked up to Anna and smiled, showing her braces. "I really love your shoes." The way she said love made it sound as if the word had twelve Vs.

"You do?" Anna croaked. She looked down at her multi-colored shoes. Was Elizabeth color blind?

Elizabeth nodded. "Where did you buy them?"

The rest of the girls surrounded Anna and Cristin, all talking at the same time. "They're so-o-o neat." One girl pulled at Cristin's arm. "What store has them?" Another girl pleaded, "I've got to have a pair."

"And I'll die if I can't have a pink pair," added Jenny.

Anna tried to explain. "I—I—"

Cristin butted in, "They're designer originals. One of a kind. Anna's got the only pair." She looked at Anna in triumph. "Tell them."

"She's right. I designed them myself."

The girls stared at Anna, then down at her shoes. Elizabeth smiled again, moving closer to Anna. "How original. Could you make me a pair?"

"And me?" The question echoed around the group of girls. Anna couldn't believe that they all wanted a pair of her crazy shoes. By the time the bell rang for second period, there were eight orders to design tennis shoes.

"I'll bring my shoes to school tomorrow," Elizabeth said. "How soon can you do them?"

Anna didn't know. "Maybe by Thursday?" How long had it taken to paint her shoes? She couldn't remember.

"And I'll need mine by Friday," Jenny called out as she left the dressing room. "For my slumber party." She turned and added, "By the way, both of you are invited."

Anna stared open-mouthed at Elizabeth and Jenny as they walked away. Then she grabbed her best friend. "Did you hear that? We're going to Jenny's party."

"I'll have to check my datebook to see if Friday is open," Cristin said.

At first, Anna thought Cristin was serious. Then she saw the dimples. The two girls practically danced all the way to orchestra class with Anna describing all the fun they were going to have.

"We'll stay up all night. I heard Jenny say something about pizza. And she said to bring all our make-up." Anna thought about the iridescent blue eye shadow she had bought last month and kept in her sock drawer. She had been saving that and some mascara her mother had given her until she was thirteen.

"And I'll bring my Beatles tapes," Cristin said. "Someone has to teach those snobs about real music."

Anna couldn't believe it. They were going to Jenny's party. And all because of her weird shoes.

Anna sat in the Pointer's living room, waiting to call out spelling words. As usual, Boots sat in her lap, licking her hand and wiggling across her legs until the dog was in its favorite position for Anna to pet her. And, as usual, Mrs. Pointer wanted to talk, asking about school and was Anna's little brother going to be a Cub Scout?

When Mark appeared, his face was screwed up in a scowl and the tops of his ears were bright red. He sat down so hard in the chair that the floor shook.

"Mark," Mrs. Pointer said.

"Sorry," he mumbled.

"Is everything set for Saturday?" his mother asked. When Mark didn't answer right away, she explained to Anna. "Mark and his father are going to play in the father-son basketball game this weekend. Mark's been practicing his shots for weeks."

Mark slouched in the corner of the chair with his hand over his eyes as if he were shading them from the sun. His bottom lip began to quiver and he wiped at his eyes with the back of his hand. Then he blurted out, "It's not fair. He cancelled our ballgame."

"Why?"

He hit at the arm of the chair. "Same old story. He has other plans."

Anna squirmed and wished that she was at home—not sitting in the Pointer's living room hearing this conversation.

Mrs. Pointer glanced at Anna as if she sensed Anna's discomfort, then looked back at Mark. "We'll talk about this later." She patted her son on the knee. "Don't let it upset you. I'll go with you to the game."

"You can't. You're not my father. It's a father and son basketball game." Mark was almost yelling at Mrs. Pointer. "Now I can't play. And everybody at school will know."

He glared at Anna and she saw that he was crying. Then, in his meanest voice, he said, "Don't you dare tell anyone what my dad did, Anna Browning. Or you'll be sorry."

Then he ran from the room.

CHAPTER NINE

O n Tuesday afternoon, Mrs. Sanders listened to Anna's etudes, alias boring—but important musical exercises. "I know you don't care for the etudes, but they are important. Practice them carefully."

As Mrs. Sanders wrote the instructions on the music, Anna tried playing the notes again. Super easy. She loved private lessons. It was much more fun to have a private lesson than to call out spelling words for Mark Pointer.

"Now let's hear the second page of your concerto. Remember to play smoothly and connected."

The music looked simple but the hard part was to play the notes connected, to keep from breaking the sound. It was like singing an entire song without stopping to take a breath. And Anna had to remember to vibrato almost every note.

"Fair," said Mrs. Sanders when Anna finished. "But your playing sounds as if you're very tired. Did you get enough sleep last night?"

Anna bowed her head. The truth was that she had been up past midnight. And if her parents found out she'd really be in hot

water. Under her bed at home sat eight pair of white tennis shoes—
actually six and a half pair that were still white. Painting three shoes
had taken hours.

When her parents thought she had gone to bed, she stuffed
a pillow along the bottom of her door so they couldn't see her
light shining. Painting other people's shoes demanded all her
concentration. Making a mistake might ruin their shoes, especially
Jenny's new pink pair.

"I was up kind of late," she confessed to Mrs. Sanders.

"We'll stop now and I'll give you a longer lesson next week,"
Mrs. Sanders said. Then she pointed her finger at Anna. "If you
promise to get to bed at a reasonable time."

"Yes ma'am."

"And Anna," the teacher said, frowning. "Your half position is
not progressing. Are you doing what I told you?"

Anna busied herself with wiping off her viola and placing it
in the case. She hadn't had time to practice as much as she needed
to—not at all yesterday. And she had to do her homework on the
bus on the way to school that morning because she spent the entire
evening painting shoes. Right now that sounded very stupid.

"I think I'm just tired," she said, crossing her fingers.

"I hope that's all. Your audition is only a week away. Be careful
of your time and make sure you practice and get plenty of rest."

Careful of her time? Between coaching Mark and painting
shoes and practicing she needed twelve extra hours in a day. And
what about tomorrow's science test? And her mother had hinted at
breakfast about 'someone' who had forgotten about her vacuuming
chore.

"One of the teachers told me that you're helping Mark with
his spelling," Mrs. Sanders said. "That's very generous of you
considering how he treats you."

"I didn't volunteer. I was drafted," Anna said. She didn't care
to explain how she had been disqualified from the spelling bee and
ended up being Mark's coach. All because she was so responsible.

The teacher laughed. "Guess it's hard to ignore someone if you have to call out spelling words to him."

Anna knew the teachers had been talking again. They didn't need eyes in the back of their heads, they simply met in the teachers' lounge and compared notes. But she hadn't forgotten that Mrs. Sanders had offered to help.

"I did try to follow your advice."

Mrs. Sanders patted her on the shoulder. "I'm sure you did. And I've noticed that you aren't always his favorite target anymore."

That was a polite way to put it, but Anna agreed. "He's nice to me at his house because his mother's there." And at school, his nasty tricks and cutting remarks were not on schedule. But she clearly remembered her shoes being tied to the chair, her book in the boys' restroom and her purse full of pencil sharpener mess. And his reaction to her question about the electric bass.

"Are you teaching him to play the electric bass?"

Mrs. Sanders looked up quickly. "Who told you that?"

"Mark did. He said his dad was going to buy him an electric bass and an amplifier. And you were going to help him so that he could play in a rock band." Anna added, "He thinks he's going to be famous."

The teacher laid her pencil down on the music stand. "Anna, I'm going to share something with you that you must promise never to repeat. Do I have your word?"

"Yes ma'am."

"Mark's parents are divorced. It's difficult for him to accept the fact that his father no longer lives with them."

Divorce. That explained why she had never seen Mark's father. Whenever she was at the Pointer's house calling out spelling words, she always thought that Mr. Pointer was at work.

Mrs. Sanders paused, looking intently at Anna before she said more. "His father sometimes promises to do things for him and then backs out. Do you understand what I'm saying?"

Anna nodded slowly, remembering yesterday's outburst. It was like a puzzle coming together. His sister's complaints last week. His dad not buying the electric bass after he had promised. And his dad canceling out of the basketball game. And Mark's tears. Except for Tommy, she had never seen a boy cry.

She tried to imagine how she'd feel if her father didn't live at home or if he backed out on a promise. Impossible. He would never do that to her. It was too horrible to think about.

Anna hurried home and dragged the vacuum cleaner out of the hall closet, roaring through the rooms, pulling and pushing the heavy machine non-stop across the carpeting until she finished. In her mad rush, she didn't move tables or chairs and completely missed the corners. Maybe her mother would be too tired to notice.

When she walked into her room and tossed books and music on the bed, the tennis shoes called silently to her. They had to be finished by Friday. Jenny and Elizabeth asked about them every day. But she ignored the shoes, taking out her viola to practice. Next week was the audition. She had to get out of half position and into All-City.

The instructions on the music suggested s-l-o-w practice so she played each note at a snail's pace. Into half position. Play the passage. Now shift back to first position. Her hand wouldn't budge. Again she tried. No luck.

But on the fifth try, it happened. She shifted smoothly into and, she couldn't believe it, out of half position. "When you can do it five times in a row," Mrs. Sanders had said, "You've got it." But a half an hour later, she didn't 'have it.' One time remained her best record. Her fingers were tired and limp and would no longer do what her brain commanded. Tomorrow, she promised herself, putting away the instrument.

That night at dinner, Anna gobbled her spaghetti quickly so she could finish painting shoes.

"Slow down, Princess," her dad said, "You got a big date tonight?"

"No, sir." She looked around at her mother and wished that she had confided with her about the shoes. She always told her mom everything. "Great spaghetti, Mom."

"Thank you. By the way, I've got the money I owe you for last week's allowance and the extra jobs," Mrs. Browning said. "I'll take you to the mall tomorrow afternoon to get your new shoes. And how about a new sweater to make up for the long wait?"

Anna shook her head. A new sweater would be great, but nobody wanted the colored tennis shoes at the mall anymore. Everyone wanted an Anna-designed pair. "Can't. I've got to coach Mark and practice. And I've changed my mind about the shoes. Mine will be OK."

"Even after you drew all over them?" Mrs. Browning asked.

Anna shrugged. "I like them." She wondered if Peter Edwards had noticed her new shoes. He had waved at her in the hall between classes that morning.

Mrs. Browning put down her fork and stared at her daughter. "But you said everybody at school would laugh at you if I made you wear them." Her parents exchanged glances then looked back at her.

"Is this our child?" her father said in a loud whisper. "Is this the same child who thought the world would come to an end if she didn't get a pair of the famous colored tennis shoes? The child who moaned and groaned? Who vowed to work her little fingers to the bone to earn money for those special shoes?"

Sometimes her dad could be so juvenile. Mr. Browning loved to tease Anna. She had once suggested that he had just emerged from the Stone Age. She didn't mean to be disrespectful, it just slipped out. Did he get mad? Nope. He bent over so that his hands almost swept the ground and did his Cro-Magnon-Caveman Man act. Right in front of Cristin. Anna thought she would croak. Cristin thought he was hilarious.

"Dad," she protested. "It's no big deal about the shoes." She thought she'd better wait to tell her mom about the designer shoes.

Cristin had taken over the business end, charging each girl three dollars. When she finished the pairs in her room, she'd be rich. "By the way, Jenny Arrington invited me to her slumber party Friday night. Can I go?"

"May I go," her mother corrected.

Mr. Browning looked at his wife in amazement. "Did Jenny invite you, too?"

Anna groaned. He never knew when to stop.

"May I?" Anna asked again, ignoring her father.

"I don't know," her mother said. She reached over and pressed her hand over Anna's forehead. "Are you feeling all right? You seem awfully pale. You're not coming down with something are you?"

"No ma'am."

Her mother inspected Anna, holding her chin and turning her head from side to side. "You're sure you're O.K.?"

Anna slipped from her mother's hold. "I'm fine. May I be excused?" She crossed her fingers. "I've got a lot of homework." Did painting shoes count as homework?

That evening, Anna sat on the floor in her room wishing that she had never seen a white tennis shoe—or a painted one. Shades of blue, purple and green stained her fingers. Stretching her hands, she worked out the cramps caused from holding the Magic Markers for the last hour. Three pairs of shoes were covered with colorful scallops, stripes, polka dots and lightening bolts—except for Jenny's pink ones.

She lived in fear of ruining Jenny's shoes. What if she made a blob instead of a star? What if her hand slipped and she ended up making a worm instead of a wiggly line? Anna knew that Jenny would take back her invitation and never speak to her again. The pink shoes were her only chance.

Her shoulders ached from bending over the shoes and her eyes burned. The digital clock on her nightstand changed numbers. Eight thirty-three. She still had to practice an hour, do her math homework and study for a social studies test. And be in bed by nine-thirty. She had promised Mrs. Sanders to get some rest.

What she really wanted to do was to crawl in the bed, pull the covers over her head and sleep for a month. At school that morning, Cristin had presented her with eleven new orders of shoes, with a promise of more to come.

A knock at her door made Anna scramble to hide the shoes.

"Telephone," said her father.

When Anna answered the phone, she sat down in surprise.

"This is Elizabeth. We're all going skating on Thursday afternoon. Do you and your friend want to come?"

"Skating?" Anna said.

"Yes, at the StarLight Skate Center." Anna could hear the impatience in Elizabeth's voice.

Anna loved skating. Although, the last time she had gone, Anna had looked like a windmill out of control as she plowed a path through the other skaters—only to land in a heap at the edge of the rink. Maybe with Elizabeth and the other girls she'd manage to be more graceful. Anna crossed fingers on both hands.

"That would be lovely," Anna said, realizing immediately how stupid she sounded. Lovely? Lovely blue and purple bruises on both knees? And she wouldn't be able to sit down comfortably for at least two days. But, yes, she was dying to go.

"My mother will drive. Where do you live?"

"She'll have to pick me at Mark Pointer's house."

"Oh, really?" Over the phone, Anna could sense Elizabeth's eyebrows raised.

"I'm coaching him for the spelling bee."

"Well, make sure you bring your skates with you."

Skates? Anna cringed. As she hung up the phone, she realized that the other girls must own their own skates. Probably the white ones with the pom-poms on each toe—not the scuffed maroon ones she'd have to rent at the rink. But now that she was Elizabeth and Jenny's friend, maybe she'd need to buy her own.

She dragged her feet all the way back to her room. Coach Mark, go skating, do homework, practice her viola and paint shoes. When was she going to get it all done? Better yet, how had she gotten into such a mess?

Taking her viola out, she started practicing her scales and working on her tone. But the notes sounded dull, lifeless and sluggish. She played the scale one more time and decided to go on to the exercises. Same problem. The etude seemed to drag on and on as she forced herself to concentrate.

Then she opened the Bach. The first section sounded a little better but her fingers felt like mashed potatoes and it was a big effort to keep the bow moving over the strings. As she approached the half position, she slowed the tempo. Shifting into half position was easy. Then she tried to shift out. Her hand locked in place and wouldn't budge.

Anna took her left hand from the instrument and shook it to get the blood flowing through her fingers before trying the half position section again. No use. Her hand locked over and over.

What had happened to yesterday's smooth shifting?

CHAPTER TEN

Lockers slammed closed as first period gym class finished dressing out. The smell of sweaty feet permeated the air as Cristin and Anna pulled on socks, laced up their P.E. shoes and drifted toward the gym.

Jenny Arrington caught up and walked between them. "Are both of you coming to my slumber party?"

"Sure," Anna said. She crossed her fingers, remembering the pink shoes. Maybe Jenny wouldn't mention them.

"And we're going skating after school tomorrow. Are you coming?"

Anna thought about the hour of practicing, the unfinished shoes and coaching Mark. Could she get it all done?

"Have you finished my shoes? I can hardly wait to see them," Jenny bubbled. "I've got a new pair of pink jeans to wear with them."

The pink shoes lay under the bed, nestled in tissue paper, still in the box. She had put off painting Jenny's shoes, afraid to make a mistake and ruin them. And she had promised to have them ready by the slumber party—Friday night. Could she afford the time to go skating?

The P.E. teacher blew her whistle and thirty-five girls lined up on the foul line for basketball team assignments. She read from the clipboard in her hand, "Elizabeth Jenkins, captain of the Yellow team. Andrea Mitchell, Red Team captain. Choose your teams, ladies." Elizabeth stepped forward and picked Jenny Arrington.

"Next she'll pick the four stooges who walk in her shadow," Cristin whispered to Anna. "And you and I will be next to last." And they always were because the popular girls were chosen first.

Anna tugged at her gym shorts. The shorts gapped so wide that her legs looked like toothpicks. She was convinced that they were sized for a two-ton Tillie—not a twelve year old. And the blouse had to be tucked in or the teacher issued demerits. She felt like someone out of her grandmother's photo album, the ones who had played field hockey in the seventeenth century.

"Anna." Elizabeth pointed at her.

Had she heard correctly? Elizabeth had never picked her before—and never right after Jenny. Why now? She stepped forward and stood beside the two girls.

After the other captain had chosen, Elizabeth called for Cristin.

"Wow," Cristin said, tugging at Anna's sleeve. "Do we dare believe it's our dynamic personalities or our athletic talent?"

Anna was so excited that she didn't care. It felt wonderful not to be the last player picked.

Basketball was not Anna's favorite sport but she played her best so as not to embarrass Elizabeth and make her sorry she had chosen her. Most of the game, Anna ran in zigzags trying to steal the ball. Twice someone stomped on her foot and her ribs ached from being elbowed. Then, in a mad scramble, the ball escaped, rolling into the boy's side of the gym.

"Go get it, Anna," Elizabeth commanded.

The boys grunted as they did push-ups, counting out loud. Anna hesitated. None of the girls ever volunteered to get a ball from the boy's side. It was too embarrassing unless you had great looking legs. And hers looked like sticks. Usually, the girls waited until the ball was tossed back. She looked at Elizabeth.

"Go on," Elizabeth said. "We don't have all day."

Not wanting to make Elizabeth mad, she ran after the ball. After all, Elizabeth was her new friend. And Friday night was the slumber party.

Just as she reached the ball, Brent Norcross saw her.

"Look at Musk in gym shorts," cried Brent, pointing. "Her legs look like a stork's—a dork stork." The other boys stopped their push-ups and stared. To Anna's horror, Peter Edwards' head popped up on the second row.

Anna prayed for the floor to swallow her or for the world to come to an end—anything to rescue her from the scene. She could ignore Brent's dumb remarks, but not with Peter watching. Grabbing the ball, she ran back across the gym, the boys' laughter following her.

Elizabeth giggled as Anna threw the ball to her. "Dork Stork. He's right. Your legs do make you look like a stork." Of course, when Elizabeth giggled, so did the four girls that always tagged along with her. And Jenny. And, except for Cristin, the rest of the class.

How could Elizabeth be so mean? Anna felt like someone had thrown the basketball into her stomach.

Cristin joined her on the sidelines. "Take my word, you do not look like a stork. But there's a distinct possibility that Elizabeth's related to a wart hog."

Her friend's joke—her real friend—made Anna feel better. Elizabeth did have beady eyes. And a big mouth.

Cristin glanced back at the boys. "I once had a dream that I was in one of the Pillsbury TV commercials and I got to punch the Pillsbury Dough Boy in the stomach." Her eyes lit up with the thought. "He looked just like Brent Norcross."

That afternoon, Mark sat across from Anna in the living room and acted as if nothing had happened yesterday. "Cartilage," Anna said. He stared at the floor. "Cartilage," she repeated. "C-a-r-t-i-l-e-g-e." He still looked at the floor, tracing a line on the rug with the toe of his tennis shoe. "Wrong. L-a-g-e." Anna circled the word on the list. She had had trouble with that one last year. She thought of the two trophies that sat on the dresser in her bedroom and how she had saved a space for a third one. Maybe it was a good thing that she wasn't eligible for junior high competition. She'd have to use a crow bar to squeeze extra time into her days to work on spelling words.

"Lieutenant."

"L-i-e-u-t-e-n-e-n-t."

"Wrong. A-n-t."

Mark didn't seem concerned that he missed two words in a row. He continued to stare at his foot as if his mind had taken a cruise to the Bahamas. He had been like that all day at school. During lunch he sat at the end of the table without joining the usual food fights and loud guffaws with his friends. In orchestra he sat on his stool and ignored Anna and Brent. Even Mrs. Sanders had asked him if he felt well.

"Antennae."

"A-n-t-."

She waited but he didn't finish the spelling. Anna was worried. Too many words were circled on the list—the same list he had zoomed through last week without missing a word.

"Forget it," he said, "I don't know that one."

"Is something wrong, Mark?"

He mimicked her in a whiney voice. "'Is something wrong?'" His voice grew louder. "What do you think is wrong, Miss Know-It-All?"

Anna waited for Mrs. Pointer to clear her throat but nothing happened. No one was going to rescue her from Mark this time. She sat up straighter and fixed a hard stare on Mark but he didn't notice.

Then she blurted out, "Why do you have to be such a bully? I just asked a simple question."

Mark looked up in surprise. Then, kicking at the rug, he dug his heel in the deep pile. "You were here yesterday. You heard what happened when my dad called."

Anna remembered. And Mrs. Sanders' explanation about the Pointer's divorce had helped her understand. Anna had thought a lot about what Mark's father had done to him.

"You probably think that I deserve not having a dad—especially a dad who always finks out on me."

"I'm sure he didn't mean to."

"He always means to." Mark nodded as if agreeing with himself. "He doesn't care. Not about me or my mom or Dana."

Anna shuffled the spelling lists. She didn't know what to say.

"He probably won't even show up for the spelling bee. And he promised that he wouldn't miss it." He kicked at the edge of the rug again. "Ah, who cares. Call out the rest of the words."

Anna looked down at the list and picked easier ones. Centipede. Leopard. Aerobics. He spelled them right. She skipped around the list finding the other ones he knew. The next eight words he got correct.

"Dessert."

"D-e-s-e-r-t."

"Wrong," she said. "Think about dessert having two s's. Like your favorite dessert and you want two helpings."

Looking up, he made a face at her, using his fingers to stretch his mouth wider and to pull his eyelids down. "That's so stupid, Musk." Then he grinned. "But thanks, that might help me remember."

Anna almost fell off the couch. Had Mark Pointer actually said thanks without his mother making him?

The garage filled with the high-pitched whine of the power saw as Mr. Browning cut through the wood, guiding the blade along the penciled line he had drawn. Risky dashed for the outside door as Anna and her little brother covered their ears. Sawdust drifted through the air, covering the top of Mr. Browning's work bench and settling in his hair.

"Get the nails, Tommy. And the hammer."

Tommy scooted off his stool and grabbed the box of nails.

"Move slowly," his dad cautioned. "If we get in a hurry, we might cause an accident." Then he showed Tommy how to hold a nail and pound it with the hammer.

"Very good. Now let's see how the other pieces fit together." As if working a giant puzzle, Mr. Browning held the pieces of wood together, guiding Tommy's hands to hold the top half, until the soapbox car materialized.

Mr. Browning winked at Anna. "Are you impressed with our work of art?"

"It's great," she said, wondering how her father could have so much patience with her hyper-active little brother. "Dad, can I ask a favor?"

He bent over the pieces and showed Tommy where to place the first nail. "Sure, Princess. What's up?"

Anna hoped he would understand what she had to ask and not tease her. "Are you busy on Saturday afternoon?"

"Are you asking me for a date?"

"Dad. Be serious. I need a favor."

"Your wish is my command, Princess."

"There's a boy in my class that needs a father," she said. "Just for Saturday afternoon so he can play in the father-son basketball game." She could hear herself and how silly she sounded. "I know how much you love to play basketball." She had already decided that if she never played the game again, it would be too soon.

Mr. Browning held Tommy's hand on the hammer, showing him how to hammer at an angle. "Dad For a Day, huh?"

"Something like that." Anna hesitated telling her father about how Mark's dad had backed out on the father-son basketball game, but knew that he deserved some kind of explanation. "His parents are divorced."

"I see." Mr. Browning stood up and faced Anna. "Basketball sounds like fun to me. Who is this lucky boy?"

"Mark Pointer. He was on your baseball team last year."

Her father helped Tommy with another nail, then moved back to let the child try to hammer alone. "Yeah, I remember. Mark was our pitcher. Nice kid. Little insensitive at times but great potential."

Insensitive? Was a rattlesnake insensitive? Anna began to have second thoughts. How many times had Mark embarrassed her in front of the orchestra class? And what about her purse? It still had pencil shavings in the bottom and he had ruined her favorite wallet. Why was she loaning him her father? After all, wasn't being his spelling coach enough?

Maybe the Magic Marker fumes had pickled her brain.

CHAPTER ELEVEN ‖

"**H**urry up, pokey," Cristin yelled at Anna as she flashed past, disappearing into the swirl of skaters that circled the rink.

Anna put her right foot into one of the maroon and gray rented skates, hoping that the last person who used them had worn clean socks—and showered regularly. On the other end of the bench, Elizabeth and Jenny were busy putting on their skates. Both girls wore skating outfits with short skirts and matching sweaters. Jenny's was pink.

"Are my shoes finished yet?" Elizabeth asked, leaning over to tie her skates.

All the way to the skating rink Anna had been dreading the question. "I'll finish them tonight and bring them to school in the morning."

Elizabeth frowned. "What's taking you so long? We've been waiting for four days."

"Sorry, but I've been practicing for the All-City Orchestra audition."

Jenny peered around Elizabeth. "Practicing what?"

"My viola," Anna answered.

Elizabeth's mouth turned down at the edges and her upper lip curled slightly. "Your viola?" The tone of her voice suggested that it must be something contagious.

Anna tried to explain but Elizabeth interrupted. "I don't care about your viola—or whatever you call it. I want my shoes."

The two girls skated off, leaving Anna sitting on the bench wondering why the afternoon wasn't turning out to be as much fun as she expected. On shaky legs, she made her way out to the rink. As Anna entered the river of skaters, gliding over the smooth wooden floor and moving to the beat of the funky music, her spirits lifted.

Cristin soon caught up with her and the girls skated side by side.

"Ladies and gentlemen," came the announcement over the loudspeakers. "It's time for a partner's dance. Choose your partner. Mixed couples only, please." The music stopped. Kids raced each other to the opening of the railing while couples began pairing up for the dance.

Anna watched as two boys claimed Elizabeth and Jenny. The foursome stood in the center of the rink, talking and waiting for the music to begin. Like sprinkled stars, a thousand tiny dots of lights speckled the skaters and the skating rink as the ball turned. As the couples danced to the slow music, Anna watched from the bleachers and wondered what it would feel like to skate with a boy. Maybe someone like Peter.

When the dance ended, the lights brightened and the waiting skaters piled back onto the rink.

An hour later, Anna's ankles ached as she groped her way around the railing of the skating rink. She looked toward the center of the rink where Elizabeth and Jenny held court. They skated in dainty circles as they talked to several boys. Jenny twirled on her pink skates, stopping to laugh at something.

"Look out," Cristin screamed as she hurled past Anna. Catching one hand on the railing, she came to an abrupt stop, almost flipping herself over the top of the rail.

"Wow," Cristin said, gasping for breath. "That's the last time I play 'Crack the Whip' with those people." She pushed her glasses back in place on her nose. "They play for keeps."

Anna resumed working her way to the opening of the railing with Cristin behind her.

"Where are you going?" Cristin demanded.

"To sit down," Anna said. "I followed Elizabeth and Jenny around the rink at least three hundred times. Then I fell and three juveniles tried to jump over me—the second one missed and landed on top of me." Anna pointed at a little kid who zoomed past them. "Before I could get up, that one tagged me and screamed 'You're it.' Right in my ear."

Even the rock'n roll that boomed over the loudspeakers couldn't lure her back onto the freeway of skaters.

"So where are Elizabeth and Jenny?" Cristin asked.

Anna pointed.

"Come on," Cristin said, reaching for Anna's arm. "Let's check out the action."

Anna squatted down to avoid Cristin's grab but Cristin was too quick. In a split second, Anna was careening through the other skaters, crouched down, one arm covering her head while Cristin pulled her across the rink. Wind whistled through Anna's hair as she peeked out at the blur of people they streaked past.

"Coming in for a landing," Cristin cried as the center of the rink loomed closer.

Anna reached out for Cristin, missed and rolled headfirst into Jenny. A swirl of pink tumbled before Anna—just before Jenny fell on top of Elizabeth. When Anna opened her eyes she could hear Cristin laughing. Elizabeth had gone down—rear end first. Jenny lay on her back, pink skates sprawled in different directions.

And beneath the tangle of arms and skates, Anna started giggling. The wild ride across the rink left her breathless. Between the gasps for breath and the giggles, she sounded like a chipmunk with the hiccups.

"Everybody OK?" Cristin asked.

"You idiots," Elizabeth screamed. "You stupid, lame-brain idiots."

Cristin stopped laughing. "I'm sorry. It was an accident." Then she snickered. "We couldn't stop."

Scrambling to her feet, Elizabeth glared at Cristin, then at Anna, who couldn't get her skates to stop slipping out from under her.

"You are both so-o-o immature." Her face grew redder as she spit out the words. Then she turned her back on them and skated off, Jenny following.

"I guess this means we need to find a ride home," Anna said as Cristin helped her up. The two girls grinned at each other. Then Anna said, "But let's go play 'Crack the Whip' one more time."

Boxes full of white tennis shoes were strewn over Anna's bed, in piles on the floor and behind the closet door. Most of the shoes were not new and the odor had escaped from the boxes, making her room smell like the school gym. Anna opened a new pack of Magic Markers and started drawing tiny red stars on Jenny's pink shoes. More green and blue. Lightening bolts and purple polka dots were added to the blue crescents and yellow daisies on the sides. She was very careful until they were finished and set out to dry.

Another pair was finished. And another. Soon four pairs were lined up on the floor beside Jenny's.

She hated sticking her hand inside the used tennis shoes, but that was the only way she could hold them up without smearing the designs. After doing each used pair, she went to the bathroom and washed her hands. It was during the third trip to the bathroom that she didn't close her bedroom door all the way.

When she returned, Tommy stood in the middle of her room. "Wow," he said. "Where did you get all the shoes?"

In Anna's panic, she didn't stop to think. She screamed, "Get out, you little monster. You're not allowed in my room." As she lunged at him, he dodged under her arm, hopped over the shoes and Magic Markers and escaped out the door.

Through the open door, Anna could hear Tommy's cries as he ran all the way to the living room. "Anna tried to hit me." And then the part Anna dreaded. "Wait until you see what's in Anna's room."

There was no time to hide the shoes.

First her mother appeared in the doorway. Then her father. Tommy the Tattler peeked out from behind their father's legs, making sure he stayed far from his sister's reach.

Anna stood in the corner, lacing and unlacing her fingers, holding her breath and waiting for her parents to explode. Her shoulders drooped and she looked at the floor. Possible punishments raced through her mind. She'd probably be confined to her room until she reached the age of twenty-one. Or sent away to reform school. And forced to scrub floors and bathrooms with a toothbrush. Or maybe worse.

Mr. Browning carefully stepped around the room, stopping to pick up a shoe and examine it, then picking up another one. Anna's mother stared at the shoes, shaking her head slowly.

"Can you explain all this?" Mr. Browning asked with a sweep of his hand.

"First Elizabeth wanted a pair . . . Then the other girls . . . But I didn't think everyone at school would."

Anna floundered through the explanation, searching for the right words. She took a deep breath. "And then Jenny invited me to her party."

"I see. At least, I think I see." He turned to Mrs. Browning. "This one's over my head. Aren't shoes your department?"

Anna's mother smiled. "Right. Why don't you and Tommy leave us alone?"

After they left, Mrs. Browning closed the door, tip-toed through the maze of shoeboxes and sat down on the bed. The silence in the room weighed heavily on Anna's shoulders as she waited for her mother to speak.

But Mrs. Browning seemed to be hypnotized as she looked at all the shoes. Finally she patted the bed beside her. "Come, sit."

Anna perched on the edge of the bed, holding her sweaty hands in her lap. It took forever for her to get up the courage to look at her mother but when she did, her mother was holding her hand over her mouth. Laughing.

"This is pretty wild, Princess."

Anna nodded in agreement.

"I bet you're the most popular girl at school?"

Anna shrugged. Then she told her mother about Jenny's slumber party and the invitation to the skating rink. She left out the part about how Elizabeth had made fun of her in P.E. class, even though the memory still lingered.

"When I was in the seventh grade, I had a little notebook with a picture of Elvis Presley on the front. Everyone wanted one." Mrs. Browning smiled. "So I spent three weeks worth of my allowance to buy a notebook for every cheerleader in the school. All twelve of them."

"Why the cheerleaders?" Anna asked.

"Because I desperately wanted to be a cheerleader." Mrs. Browning tucked Anna's hair behind her ears as they talked. "I wanted to dress like them, talk like them. And I wanted to run out at the pep rallies and do somersaults. Just like the cheerleaders."

"And? What happened?"

It was her mother's turn to shrug. "I've forgotten. But I remember that at the time, it was very important to me." Mrs. Browning picked up one of Jenny's pink shoes and examined it, turning it around. "Nice work." Then she looked at Anna and grinned. "Maybe I should order a pair."

Anna grinned back.

"Next questions," her mother said. "Have you done your homework?"

Anna nodded.

"Practiced?"

Anna nodded again. "I did that first."

"Good for you. Now, young lady, no more shoe decorating until after your audition. Promise?"

Breathing a sigh of relief, Anna gladly promised. Thank goodness, no reform school.

"I know that the shoes are important but so is the audition," her mother said. "You'll have to decide which is most important." Mrs. Browning gave Anna a hug, then stood up and walked to the door. "And you have exactly ten minutes to pick up all these shoes and get into bed. No more lights on after bedtime. Understand?"

"Yes ma'am."

After her mother closed the door, Anna sprawled across her bed, relieved that she wasn't grounded for a year. Or more. She flipped her hair back over her ears. Even though she wasn't in trouble, she wished she hadn't hollered at Tommy. She should have tried bribing him with money or a couple of chocolate bars. Maybe he wouldn't have snitched. Nope, he would have stuffed the money in his space cadet bank, eaten the chocolate and then told on her. Just like Mark Pointer did when he threw her science book in the boys' restroom.

Maybe, in the near future, if her luck turned, the gypsies would steal him. Not her little brother. Mark Pointer.

CHAPTER TWELVE ‖

As the orchestra rehearsed the *Brandenburg*, Anna fought to keep up with the brisk tempo. It was Friday and all the late nights of painting shoes and practicing had caught up with her. Her fingers felt like rubber. Instead of working like hammers, they collapsed and wobbled regardless of what her brain told them to do.

Anna concentrated so hard on keeping her fingers moving that she forgot about the half position. As usual, she shifted and played the half position segment of the music. Then she shifted back! Her hand moved with the same fluid motion as the other violists. She was so excited that she wiggled in her chair as she played.

While Mrs. Sanders coached the first violins on a tricky section in their part, Anna silently 'ghost' played the section again. She didn't need sound to tell that the shift was smooth. She tried again. But the third time, her hand locked in place. And again the fourth time. Her excitement fizzled.

When class ended, Mrs. Sanders winked at Anna. "All your hours of practicing are paying off." The teacher smiled proudly. "I'm expecting an outstanding audition on Monday."

Butterflies took flight in Anna's stomach. Three more days. Could she do it? Her goal was to be able to shift smoothly five times in a row. Sweat popped out in her palms. Five seemed like an impossible number.

She and Cristin picked up their instruments and started out the door.

"I saw Elizabeth and Jenny wearing their 'Anna-Designed' shoes this morning," Cristin said. "Was Elizabeth still mad?"

Anna shrugged. "I gave them their shoes and Elizabeth said something about me being slow. But not a word about yesterday."

Cristin's dimples danced as she grinned. "I wish I had had my camera at the skating rink. She looked so funny. I'll bring my camera tonight—just in case. What time are you leaving for the slumber party?"

"I don't know. I have to go to Mark's house after school. Then I have to practice." Her schedule had improved after her parents discovered the shoes. But the audition was only three days away and she was worried. If she practiced this afternoon, twice on Saturday, twice on Sunday . . . was that enough time?

When they passed Brent Norcross in the hall, he started shouting. "Musk alert, Musk alert." Then the fat boy grinned at her. "That's the new alarm to warn everyone that you're approaching. Like it?"

Without hesitating, Anna stepped forward until her nose was almost touching Brent's and her balled-up fist was under his chin.

"This is my new Brent alert. Want to feel it?"

Brent ducked into math class without another 'Musk alert.'

"Your Brent alert works well," Cristin said, her eyes twinkling and growing larger behind her classes. "See you tonight." She waved at Anna before following the Pillsbury Dough Boy into class.

Anna stood a little taller as she walked down the hall, hugging her books tightly.

"Anna—wait up." She turned to see Peter Edwards running down the hall to catch up with her. "Are you ready for the audition?" he asked.

She felt her cheeks grow warm as she shook her head. Last night she had managed to play the *Brandenburg* correctly three times in a row. And again today. But three times was no guarantee that she could play the passage right by Monday. Sometimes her shifting worked and sometimes it didn't.

"You really sound great," he said. "I heard you warming up before class began."

Vaguely aware of the people who turned to stare at them, Anna floated down the hall beside Peter. Why had he been listening to her play? Did that mean he liked her? She glanced sideways at him. He was very cute. And she loved his big blue eyes and his cocky grin.

"Mind if I come to the audition?" he asked. "Or would it make you too nervous? After all, you were nice enough to come to mine."

Anna's tongue stuck to the roof of her mouth. Why did dumb things happen to her every time Peter talked to her? She managed to get her lips moving and answer him. "Sure."

"And maybe you'd like to ride with me to the All-City rehearsal Monday night. My mom can drive. We live a couple of blocks from your house."

The butterflies took flight again and Anna found it hard to breathe. He had already assumed that she would pass the audition. And he knew where she lived. She wished she knew what all this meant.

"See you on Monday," Peter said, waving as he disappeared into science class.

Anna walked the rest of the way to language arts class in a trance. Dumb me, she thought, I managed to say exactly one word during the entire conversation. Had Peter noticed?

"Elocution."
"E-l-o-c-u-t-i-o-n."

"Hippopotamus."

"H-i-p-p-o-p-o-t-a-m-u-s."

Mark pushed her to call out the words faster and faster. He perched on the edge of his chair, leaning forward with his elbows on his knees. He seemed to spell the words before they left Anna's mouth.

"Metropolitan."

"M-e-t-r-a-p-o-l-i-t-a-n."

When Anna told him he was wrong, Mark beat at his knee with his fist. "That was stupid. That's the easiest word on the whole list." He pressed his lips together and glared at Anna. "Give me another word. Hurry."

She flipped through the pages in her hand. They had exhausted four word lists, plus a high school list, and her throat hurt from calling out words. When she first arrived at the Pointer's house, she expected Mark to say something about her dad. Maybe thanks? Or whatever someone is supposed to say when you let him them borrow your father. But he didn't mention the game or Mr. Browning and neither did Anna. Never again, she thought. Next time he's on his own.

"Get with it, Musk," he commanded.

Anna looked up at the grandfather clock in the corner. She had been at Mark's house for over an hour. An empty plate sat on the coffee table where Mrs. Pointer had left pecan cookies. Anna's mother would be putting dinner on the table soon. And she was due at Jenny's slumber party by seven-thirty that evening.

"My name is not Musk and I'm going home," she said, putting the lists in order and handing them to Mark.

He grabbed her arm hard. "You can't go. The spelling bee is Tuesday morning." He fished behind him and pulled out more lists. "Call out these."

"I'm going home," she repeated. "Call out your own words."

"All right, all right. We still have Monday afternoon left."

Anna stared at him open mouthed. How could he be so dense?

"For your information, Mr. Pointer, I have a very important audition on Monday afternoon." She stood over Mark and shook her finger at him. "And if I don't pass the audition it'll be partly your fault because I spent so much time calling out your dumb spelling words."

Mark seemed to shrink back against his chair.

"And another thing," she said, practically spitting out the words at him. "I'm tired of you picking on me at school. No more. Do you hear me?"

He held his hands up in defense. "I hear you."

She gathered up her books and coat, then walked over in front of his chair again. This time she leaned so close that their noses almost touched—just like she had done to Brent that morning. "And don't ever call me 'Musk' again. Not at school. Not at All-City. Never. And you'd better warn your little friend Brent Norcross that I mean business."

Just as Anna opened the front door, Mrs. Pointer entered the room. "Mark, escort Anna to the door and don't forget to tell her how much you appreciate all her help. She's given you a lot of her time in the last two weeks." Then Mrs. Pointer winked at Anna.

Mark walked out the door behind Anna and mumbled his usual thanks. "Can you come over tomorrow? We can work after the basketball game."

Anna looked straight into Mark's eyes. "No. Capital N-O." She was tired of calling out spelling words, tired of Mark the Tyrant and tired of painting everyone's tennis shoes.

"And, by the way, you're welcome," she added.

"For what?

"For the loan of my father."

After practicing her private lesson assignment, Anna tackled the *Brandenburg*. Warming up the fingers and brain was very important before playing real music. Very slowly, her fingers moved through the half position passage, her hand shifting smoothly. Twice. Three times. But a knock at her bedroom door interrupted the fourth attempt.

"It's after seven," her mother said. "Are you ready for me to drive you to Jenny's?"

The *Brandenburg* stared back at her. Monday was the audition.

"Not yet," she said. "I'll have to be late."

Trying a faster tempo, she started practicing again. The piece seemed infinitely easier than it had two weeks ago. Her intonation sounded polished, her bowing precise and controlled. Remembering the dynamics had become natural as she played the *fortes*, *pianos* and *crescendos*. And the shifting no longer intimidated her.

Glancing at the clock, she noted the time and kept practicing. By eight-thirty, the record of shifting correctly stood at four. Four times. With two more days to practice, she might meet her goal by Monday's audition. Might was a very frightening word. Stretching her arms, she decided to take a break.

She found her mother in the living room, reading the newspaper.

"Ready to go to Jenny's?" Mrs. Browning asked.

Anna chewed on her bottom lip. "I'm not going." She had not thought about staying at home. It just popped into her brain. And it made a lot of sense. "I think I'll go to bed early tonight."

Her mother folded the paper and put it beside her. "You've been working pretty hard this week."

The week had been the hardest of Anna's entire life. She barely had time to breathe and now she was so tired that her legs felt like they were filled with lead. Did she dare tell her mother how stupid she had been? Would she understand how Anna had jeopardized her big chance at All-City by wasting time painting tennis shoes?

Mrs. Browning motioned for Anna to come sit by her. "Things have been a little rough lately, haven't they?"

Anna nodded and looked down at her hands.

"How's the practicing? You sounded pretty terrific to me."

Even if she played like a beginner, her mother would tell her that her music sounded great. "Better. I think I've got a good chance if I work hard over the weekend."

Mrs. Browning smiled. "How about if I give Tommy all your jobs, like taking out the garbage and vacuuming this weekend? That way, you would be free to practice and rest—unless you're going to the basketball game tomorrow?"

"No way." Anna's eyes snapped open. "I wouldn't go across the street to see Mark Pointer. Not even if you paid me."

Before she realized what she was saying, all the stories about Mark—the spelling bee, her shoes tied to the chair, the pencil shavings in her purse, and even the time that he put two-sided tape on her chair in orchestra—rolled out of her mouth. And to her surprise, Anna and her mother were soon laughing at the stories, especially the one about her science book in the boys' restroom.

"It's tough being twelve," Mrs. Browning said, tucking Anna's hair behind one ear and giving her a hug. "It must have been a hard decision not to go tonight," she said softly. "I'm very proud of you."

Somehow, Anna sensed that her mother understood about the shoes. And Elizabeth and Jenny. And especially Mark. As she walked back to her room, she made two decisions. No more painting shoes—even after the audition. No more letting Mark bully her.

When her little brother burst into her room, Anna was snuggled among her stuffed animals, reading a book. Her first impulse was to yell at him but then she remembered the last time he had visited her room.

"You're supposed to knock, you little pest," she said.

He stuck out his tongue at her. "Mom says you're wanted on the phone, weirdo."

When she answered the phone, Cristin's voice screamed at her so loud that Anna had to hold the receiver away from her ear. "Why didn't you tell me you weren't going to Jenny's party? I show up and wait and wait for you. What happened?"

Anna felt guilty that she had stood up her best friend—possibly her only real friend. "I forgot to call you," she admitted. "I decided to stay at home and practice. The audition is on Monday."

"Well, I wouldn't have wasted my time if I had known you weren't coming."

"Are you having fun?"

"Fun? Is swimming with piranhas fun? Lisa ate too much pizza and got sick and threw up all over Jenny's pink canopied bed. Then Elizabeth got mad at Laurie because Laurie likes David Richardson. And Elizabeth said that she liked him first. Anyway, I told Jenny's mother that I felt like throwing up. She called my mom and I came home early."

"Are you still sick?"

"Get serious. I got sick of Elizabeth and Jenny. They're flakes. Jenny's an air head and Elizabeth is a barracuda."

"Yeah, I know," Anna said. But she had been awfully slow to learn.

"Want to go to the mall tomorrow? I'm getting a new hamster."

CHAPTER THIRTEEN

On Monday morning, Anna dressed out for P.E. class, sat on the fourth row of the gym bleachers and waited for Cristin who was still searching for her gym socks. Counting on her fingers, Anna calculated that there were six and a half hours until the audition. She still had to suffer through orchestra, social studies, language arts, math and biology. Then the audition. The mention of the word "audition" made her stomach roll over and play dead. Forget about eating lunch.

As the girls' gym class lined up and started answering roll call, Cristin hopped out of the dressing room, pulling on one shoe and trying to lace it up at the same time.

"Some wise guy stuffed my socks between the lockers," she said to Anna as she took her place in line. "Look at them. They look like they were used for a tug of war." And they did. The tops were so stretched that Cristin could get two feet in one sock if she tried. "Gross. What kind of disease can you catch from dirty socks?"

"Probably something that you have to take shots for," Anna said, remembering the rented roller skates.

"I just hope no one wore them," Cristin said. "Who won the father-son basketball game?"

Anna shrugged. "It was a tie. But my father loved it. He even took Mark out for hamburgers after the game."

"Are you serious? Your dad needs his head examined."

Anna answered roll call and began biting at her fingernail. How many hours had she practiced over the weekend? By Sunday afternoon she could shift smoothly five times in a row but last night she could only manage three times. She needed more days to practice but the conductor was scheduled to hear her play today.

When the teacher called for the basketball team captains, Elizabeth and Andrea stepped forward.

"Choose your teams, ladies," the teacher said.

At first Anna didn't pay attention to the names being called. Her mind wandered as she daydreamed about the audition. She stood before the conductor who glared at her, unsmiling, unsympathetic. When she tried to shift, her hand was stuck to the viola with Super Glue. She couldn't move her fingers or her hand. And Mrs. Sanders and Peter were laughing at her.

Shaking her head to clear the vision, she turned to tell Cristin that she couldn't go through with the audition. But Cristin was gone. All the girls had been picked for the teams but Anna and Lucy Matthews, the slowest runner in the class. Lucy was always the last girl to be picked. Behind Andrea, Cristin knelt on the floor, pulling up her wilted socks and tying her other shoe.

Elizabeth looked right through Anna as if she was invisible. "I'll take Lucy."

As the two teams assembled on opposite ends of the court, Anna stood beside Cristin and watched Elizabeth issue orders to her team. "Looks like things are back to normal," Anna said, grinning.

"Thank goodness," Cristin said, pulling up her socks again.

"Let's work on the *Brandenburg*," said Mrs. Sanders to the orchestra class.

Anna's heart froze. Why did they have to rehearse that piece today of all days? She loved the Bach but didn't want to play the piece too many times before the audition. What if she used up all her shifting in class? She fished through her folder and found the piece. It had been brand new when Mrs. Sanders first gave it to the orchestra. Now, pencil marks covered the page with fingerings, bowings and additional symbols to remind Anna to play soft or loud. And the measures of half position were circled. Putting the viola under her chin, Anna waited for Mrs. Sanders' downbeat.

"Pretend that this is our concert," Mrs. Sanders suggested. "Give me lots of sound and energy."

The crisp style of the piece sparkled as the students played, bows moving perfectly together, fingers working like little pistons. As the melody line left the violins, the violas picked it up and carried it, passing it to the cellos. The joy of making music united the class until the orchestra sounded like one giant instrument.

"Bravo," said Mrs. Sanders when the piece finished.

Anna leaned back in her chair. She had been so caught up in the music that she didn't even notice the half position section. She played with a new enthusiasm that came from knowing the piece so well that a deeper enjoyment of the music took over. But how many times could she play the piece without her hand locking?

Somehow Anna suffered through the rest of the morning, thinking only of one thing: the audition. She barely passed a pop quiz in social studies because her concentration kept wandering.

Later, when the language arts teacher called on her to answer a question, she jumped in her chair as if someone had pinched her. And the entire class laughed.

Her lunch tray sat in front of her, the meat loaf getting cold and hard, the rice turning to a blob of starch. How could she possibly eat when her stomach felt like a punching bag? Even her Nutty Buddy ice cream cone was melting. Every time the audition crossed her mind, her stomach twisted and her hands started sweating.

"Hey, Anna. Can I have your roll? I'll trade you my carrot salad," Brent asked from his end of the table.

She shoved the entire tray toward him. "Take everything. Help yourself."

He scraped the food onto his own tray, then sent her empty one back down the table. Whether the meat loaf was cold or hot, didn't seem to bother Brent as he chopped up the meat, mixed it with the rice and wolfed it down. The ice cream disappeared into his mouth without a single drip on his hand.

"Disgusting," Cristin said, looking away from Brent, who was licking his fingers. "No wonder he's shaped like an elephant." But Anna didn't hear her. She was in never-never land, auditioning again.

Cristin banged on the table top with her open palm. "Come in world."

When Anna looked up, Cristin said, "This is your best friend, the voice of experience speaking. Stop worrying about the audition. You'll be great."

But Anna only stared back at her.

"Look, an audition is like going to the dentist," Cristin said. "The worst part is the waiting."

Elizabeth and Jenny paraded past the two girls, their four 'shadows' following close behind. They all wore new suede boots. Anna thought the shoes made their feet look fat.

"Hey, I forgot to tell you about Nibbles," Cristin said, grabbing her arm. "You won't believe what happened."

"Nibbles?"

"The new hamster, putty-brain. Remember the cute little furry animal you helped me pick out at the mall? The one you almost dropped in the hermit crab cage?"

Anna shook her head. "I don't care about your hamster." She pointed to her watch. "I have two hours before I audition. I'm dying of stage fright and you want to talk about hamsters. Give me a break."

Cristin's eyes widened at her friend's outburst.

Anna held her hands out to her best friend. "What if I don't play well?"

"Aw, you'll do fine. Don't worry. Dr. Giacomo is a pussy cat."

"The conductor? But you said he yelled at the orchestra. What if he yells at me?" And Anna remembered the picture in the violin repair shop. He really looked mean.

Cristin shook her head. "You weren't listening—as usual. I said that he yelled at the flute player. She played the wrong note five times in a row. She's a real pin-head. So Dr. Giacomo got mad and yelled at her. Could you blame him?"

"I guess not." But even Cristin's explanation didn't help. Anna had seen the poster at the violin shop.

"Now would you like to hear about Nibbles?"

"If you insist. What happened to this hamster?"

"Well, you remember the big clear, plastic ball that we bought for Nibbles?"

Anna nodded. The ball had been about the size of a volleyball and was hinged around the middle. The idea was to put a hamster inside and let him exercise by running and making the ball roll around on the floor. But Anna had had to go home before Cristin tried putting Nibbles in his new toy.

"I was watching him roll around the living room. You know? And the phone rang—it was that dumb boy in my math class wanting to know what page our homework was on. Anyway, while I was on the phone, my mother left the front door open when she went to get the newspaper. And Nibbles rolled out. We haven't seen him since. He's probably still rolling through town."

Anna tried not to laugh but she couldn't stop. It really wasn't funny, that poor little hamster peddling his way across town, but, she thought, it would make a great movie.

"A smile," Cristin said, throwing her arms into the air. "Don't you feel much better?"

But the feeling didn't last long. As she carried her lunch tray to the window and their class lined up to leave the lunchroom, Anna felt her knees tremble. Cristin poked her in the back. "Relax, silly. You spent the entire weekend practicing. I'm telling you—you'll be great."

True, she had practiced for over two hours both on Saturday and Sunday. Her playing sounded better than ever but what about all those hours she wasted painting shoes? If she didn't make All-City, she could only blame it on her own stupidity.

CHAPTER FOURTEEN ‖

At the end of seventh period, the last bell rang and the student stampede moved down the hall toward the waiting yellow school buses. Anna trailed behind them, not bothering to step in the middle of the floor tiles as the students passed her. She needed more than luck to pass the audition. Stepping on cracks had lost their power.

Mrs. Sanders looked up as Anna walked into the orchestra room. "Go ahead and get your instrument out and be warming up. We'll be with you in a minute." Then she continued her conversation with Dr. Giacomo, who sat exactly where he had for Peter's audition. Maybe Cristin was wrong, Anna wondered. With those piercing black eyes, Dr. Giacomo still looked awfully cruel to her.

The orchestra room seemed larger than usual without students. Empty chairs and music stands had been straightened for tomorrow's class. Someone had erased the chalkboard where Mrs. Sanders had written the date of Mozart's birthday.

And it was very quiet. Too quiet.

The viola felt cold in Anna's hand. She tightened the bow and played the open strings softly to see if they were in tune. In the

stillness of the room, she sounded awfully loud. Turning her back
to Mrs. Sanders and the conductor, she tried a scale. Play in tune .
. . smooth bowing . . . tone quality, all the things that Mrs. Sanders
always reminded her to concentrate on, raced through her head.
Was Dr. Giacomo grading her on her warm-up?

She played the Bach very slowly. Once, twice. Then she stopped.
Her shifting was smooth and even, but she didn't want to tire her
hand before the actual audition.

The door opened and Cristin and Peter came in, sitting on the
back row. Cristin waved and Peter grinned at her. All Anna could
manage in return was a tiny smile.

She could hear her best friend telling Peter about her new
hamster. "I've looked all over the neighborhood for the little
booger."

Anna's clammy hands began to sweat as she played through
another piece. An entire audience. Her parents had wanted to come
to school for the audition but Anna refused. Too many people
make me nervous, she had told them. What would they think if
they knew that half the world was already in the room?

"Do you think the police will pick up Nibbles? Maybe I should
get my mother to call them when I get home," Cristin whispered
loudly.

Forcing herself to stop listening to Cristin, Anna stared at the
music.

"Are you ready?" Mrs. Sanders asked.

Anna's stomach gave a lurch. It was time. She walked to the
front of the room and placed her music on the stand.

Mrs. Sanders spoke again. "Anna, I'd like you to meet Dr.
Giacomo, the conductor of the All-City Youth Orchestra."

The conductor stood and held out his hand for Anna to shake.
"I'm looking forward to hearing you play," he said with a smile.
When Anna finally gathered the courage to look at him, his brown
eyes were warm and friendly. Luckily, she remembered to wipe her
sweaty palms on her jeans before shaking hands with him.

"How about playing a C scale first," Mrs. Sanders said.

From the back of the room, Cristin gave her the thumbs up sign for good luck and Peter said, "Break a leg."

C Major. Anna silently reviewed the key signature for C Major before playing. No sharps, no flats. Her fingers were still damp even after wiping them on her jeans. She played, thinking about finger patterns, watching her bow and listening to make sure each note was in tune.

"Excellent," Mrs. Sanders said. "And now the Bach."

Anna glanced at the music and panicked. The notes on the music seemed foreign. Nothing looked familiar. Had she picked up the wrong music? She checked the title. *Brandenburg Concerto No. 3* by Johann Sebastian Bach. The pencil marks and the finger numbers were hers. The corner was taped where Brent Norcross had torn it. It was her music. Slowly she felt the familiarity return.

"You may begin anytime you're ready, Anna."

How about in the next century, Anna thought. She carefully placed her bow on the string but it skidded, making funny sounds. She glanced at Dr. Giacomo.

"We'll overlook that solo," the conductor said, smiling. "I don't think Bach wrote any notes that were supposed to sound like that."

From the back of the room, Cristin giggled, trying to hide the sound behind her hand.

Anna took a deep breath and tried to put her bow on the string again. This time her control returned and the real notes rang out. She played the opening section with confidence. On the running eighth notes she remembered to get louder, then softer. She remembered to keep the style crisp and clean.

As the half-position measures got closer, her hand gripped the viola tighter and tighter. Five more measures. Relax, she told herself. Three more measures. You can do it, she told herself. One more measure. She shifted into half-position and played the section. Then, without hesitating or slowing down, she shifted back into first position—smoothly.

She finished the piece and put her instrument in rest position as Cristin and Peter jumped to their feet and started cheering. They surrounded her, patting her on the back and hopping up and down.

"You did it," yelled Peter.

"I knew you could!" shouted Cristin.

Anna felt as if her heart would burst. Even though she was nervous, even though her hands sweated, even though she wasn't thirteen yet, she had escaped the half position trap.

The three students turned to Dr. Giacomo.

He pulled out a large black folder from his brief case. On the front in beautiful gold letters was printed "All-City Symphony Youth Orchestra." He handed it to Anna. "Congratulations, Anna. I think you'll need this tonight at rehearsal."

Opening the folder, Anna looked at all the music. Beethoven. Rossini. Brahms. She could hardly wait for the first rehearsal.

"You'll need to be measured for a new uniform," Mrs. Sanders said. "And don't make any plans for Spring Break. You'll be going to Disney World with the orchestra."

Peter nodded. "We're going to have a blast."

Anna put her viola in the case and all her music inside the new folder.

"Don't forget," Dr. Giacomo said with a wink. "Rehearsal's tonight at seven."

Anna grinned at him and nodded. "Yes, sir." She couldn't imagine him ever yelling at anyone.

As the three students walked down the hall, Peter reminded Anna that she was riding to the rehearsal with him. And Cristin babbled about being roommates when they went to Disney World. But Anna hugged the music folder to her chest, re-living the audition. All the hours of practice had come together. She felt as if she could play the Bach two hundred times without a mistake.

"See you tonight," Peter said as he headed for his mother's car.

Anna wanted to run and shout to the sky that she had passed the audition. But instead she grabbed Cristin and they jumped up and down, sharing her excitement.

"I can't believe it," Anna said.

"I told you that you could do it," Cristin answered, her dimples growing deeper and deeper.

Anna took Cristin's arm and started walking down the sidewalk. "Are you really going to call the police about Nibbles?"

Cristin started laughing so hard that she dropped her books. "Boy, did you swallow that story." She pointed at Anna and laughed again. "I made up the whole story to keep your mind off the audition. Nibbles is safe at home in his cage."

Then Cristin quickly grew serious. "I hope."

CHAPTER FIFTEEN ||

The auditorium buzzed with voices. Extra chairs lined the aisles as students were herded into their assigned seats. In the first three rows sat the mayor, two councilmen, the school superintendent and an assortment of parents. A photographer from the newspaper wandered around the edge of the stage, checking the lighting and changing the lens on her camera. Eight chairs and a microphone sat on the stage.

Sitting in the auditorium with her homeroom class, Anna didn't feel the slightest regret that she wasn't in the spelling bee. Last night's rehearsal with the All-City Orchestra had been perfect. She had a little trouble with some of the music but practice would take care of that. The scariest part came when the conductor introduced her to the orchestra and she managed to stand up without falling on her face or doing anything stupid. And no one laughed at her. Peter's mother had even taken them out for chocolate shakes afterward to celebrate.

"Here comes Mr. Personality himself," Cristin said, nudging Anna in the ribs. The spelling contestants started marching down the aisle and up the steps to the empty chairs. Anna almost didn't recognize Mark. He wore a navy blue suit and a bright red tie. And his hair looked like it had been plastered down with hair spray.

"He looks like the geek of the week." Cristin said as he walked by the girls. "I hope he bombs out. Maybe losing would teach him a lesson."

Anna didn't answer her. She stretched her neck to watch the parents who entered from the back of the auditorium.

"Maybe when he walks up the steps, he'll trip and break his nose." Cristin giggled. "Or his mouth. That would fix him."

The seventh grade boys cheered for Mark as he mounted the stage steps. "Hey-hey, Marko." Jody Daniels managed one whistle before the homeroom teacher pounced on him and marched him off to the discipline office.

"So much for his fan club," Cristin said.

After Saturday's basketball game, Anna's dad had announced at dinner that he planned to bring a big surprise to the spelling bee—for Mark. She couldn't believe that her dad had actually liked Mark and wanted to do something nice for him. But then, her father had never acted normal.

When she saw him enter the auditorium, she immediately recognized his big surprise. As Mr. Browning sauntered down the aisle, grinning and swinging his arms as if he were the guest of honor, Anna knew why Mark Pointer didn't look anything like his mother. He looked exactly like his father—who now walked beside Mr. Browning.

Mr. Browning leaned over the row as he passed the girls. "What's cookin', good lookin'?" Then he gave them a big wink. Anna turned six shades of red and wished her chair would fold up and swallow her. Would her father ever grow up? He straightened and waved at Mark who stared open-mouthed at both fathers.

"What is your father doing with Mark's father?" Cristin asked.

Anna reluctantly explained again about the basketball game. This time she admitted that it was her idea that her dad take Mark.

"His dad sometimes disappoints him," she said, sounding like Mrs. Sanders.

Cristin held her hand to Anna's forehead as if checking for a fever. "Have you gone batty? That guy goes out of his way to make life miserable for you. And you want to loan him your father?"

"I felt sorry for him." And she did. Mark wasn't as tough as he acted.

"I think you've been painting too many shoes. It's warped your brain."

Finally the program began. First, the principal, Mr. Meeham, tapped and blew into the microphone to see if it was working. It was. Then he introduced all the important visitors and welcomed the parents.

Anna sneaked a peek at her father. Just as she suspected, he sat up very straight, smiling and looking at her out of the corner of his eye. He seemed extremely proud of himself.

Next, Mr. Meeham introduced the newscaster from the local television station who was to call out the spelling words. Everybody applauded and craned their necks for a better view of the local celebrity who wore a plaid sports coat and a red tie—exactly like Mark's. Then the principal introduced the teacher in charge of the dictionary. The applause for her was short-lived.

The match began.

The eight students sat stiffly in their chairs, each dressed in their Sunday best clothes. Each student spelled their words correctly for the first five rounds. Then the words got harder. Rhetoric. Caisson. Three students missed and dropped out of the competition. Antennae. Hippopotamus.

Anna knew the spelling words so well that she could tell from which list they had been selected.

Two more rounds and the finalists had narrowed to four students.

"Thyroid," said the TV newscaster.

One student missed and it was Mark's turn.

"Come on, Mark," Anna said silently as he stood to spell.

"Thyroid, T-h-y-r-o-i-d. Thyroid."

"Correct."

The three students looked more nervous than ever as the newscaster shuffled his papers. On the word "phenomenon" one boy missed and two students were left, Mark and a girl with long blonde hair and glasses.

Four rounds and neither missed a word. Five rounds. Six. The word "Britannica" went to the girl.

"Britannica. B-r-i-t-a-n-i-c-a. Britannica."

"Incorrect. Mark Pointer?"

Mark stepped up to the microphone with a smug grin. "Britannica. B-r-i-t-a-n-n-e-c-a. Britannica."

"Incorrect. Since both contestants missed, we go on to the next word."

Cristin whispered in Anna's ear, "Look at the stupid expression on his face. He thought he had won."

And Anna had thought he had won when she heard the word. How could he blow it on a word he knew? All those wasted afternoons flashed through her mind. How could he do this to her?

The announcer cleared his throat. The new word was given to the blonde-headed girl first. "Stationery," he said into the microphone.

"Stationary, S-t-a-t-i-o-n-a-r-y. Stationary."

"I'm sorry but that's incorrect. Mark Pointer? Stationery."

Anna tightened her fists and leaned forward. "Ask for the definition, dummy," she whispered. "She spelled the wrong word."

Mark looked at the girl then at the announcer.

Anna almost groaned out loud, knowing that Mark didn't understand why the girl had missed the word. She wanted to run up on stage and shake him until his teeth rattled. Ask for the definition, she prayed.

Mark looked out to the audience to where Anna sat. She sent mental waves to him. Ask for the definition. Ask for the definition. Ask for the definition . . . .

"Could I please have the definition?"

Anna was in shock. He had actually said, "Please."

He listened to the teacher slowly read the definition and then said, "Stationery. S-t-a-t-i-o-n-e-r-y. Stationery."

"Correct. Ladies and gentlemen, the new district spelling bee champion, Mark Pointer of Lincoln Junior High School."

As applause broke out, the students stood up, cheering for Mark. Some of the kids stomped on the floor but the teachers didn't seem to mind. In the midst of the noise, gold trophies were brought out and given to the third and second place winners. And, as the students in the audience continued to stand and applaud, the newscaster presented the largest trophy to Mark.

Anna grinned proudly at her dad, feeling as if she had won herself. She was really glad that Mark was the new champion. But next year, she promised herself, when I'm thirteen, Mark won't have a chance.

The principal motioned for the photographer to come up on stage and the three winners lined up, Mark in the middle. But suddenly Mark stepped out of the line and tugged at the principal's sleeve, whispering in his ear.

Mr. Meeham went to the microphone and announced, "Will Anna Browning please come up on stage? It seems that Anna was Mark Pointer's coach and he has asked that she be included in the picture."

Cristin squealed in her ear as Anna started to stand up. "I can't believe it. He's actually human."

The winners opened ranks to allow Anna to stand beside Mark. He shifted his trophy until it was between them. "You hold half of it," Mark said. "You did half the work."

Anna's mouth dropped open in surprise—just as the photographer took the picture.